There's a Girl in My Hammerlock

with Related Readings

Glencoe
McGraw-Hill

New York, New York   Columbus, Ohio   Woodland Hills, California   Peoria, Illinois

Acknowledgments

Grateful acknowledgment is given authors, publishers, photographers, museums, and agents for permission to reprint the following copyrighted material. Every effort has been made to determine copyright owners. In case of any omissions, the Publisher will be pleased to make suitable acknowledgments in future editions.

There's A Girl in My Hammerlock by Jerry Spinelli. This edition is reprinted by arrangement with Simon & Schuster Books For Young Readers, Simon & Schuster Children's Publishing Division. Copyright © 1991 by Jerry Spinelli. All rights reserved.

"'Just Another Wrestler': She Makes Her Mark in Male-Dominated Sport" by Eric Anderson, Wisconsin State Journal. Copyright © 2000 Madison Newspapers. Reprinted by permission.

"68 Teams Compete in Iditarod" by Mary Pemberton. Reprinted with permission of The Associated Press.

From *First in the Field: Baseball Hero Jackie Robinson* by Derek T. Dingle. Copyright © 1998 Derek T. Dingle, reprinted by permission of Hyperion Books for Children.

"jackie robinson" from *An Ordinary Woman*, by Lucille Clifton. Copyright © 1974 by Lucille Clifton. Reprinted by permission of Curtis Brown, Ltd.

"Offspring" by Naomi Long Madgett. Reprinted by permission of the author.

"The Journey" from *Dream Work* by Mary Oliver. Copyright © 1986 by Mary Oliver. Used by permission of Grove/Atlantic, Inc.

Cover Art: *Girl and Geranium*, Fairfield Porter, 1963, Christie's Images

Note: *Characters and events in this novel depict an issue in many communities today—that of gender-neutral selection for athletic teams. Some words, phrases, references, or situations may offend certain readers.*

Glencoe/McGraw-Hill
A Division of The **McGraw·Hill** Companies

Send all inquiries to:
Glencoe/McGraw-Hill
8787 Orion Place
Columbus, OH 43240

ISBN 0-07-826016-7
Printed in the United States of America
1 2 3 4 5 6 7 8 9 026 04 03 02 01

Contents

There's a Girl in My Hammerlock

Continued

Contents *Continued*

There's a Girl in My Hammerlock

Jerry Spinelli

March 22

Dear Editor,
   It seems like half the people in town
have written to you about me. And of
course, you and your reporters have done
a lot too. Headlines. Stories. Photos.
Sometimes I think if it wasn't for me,
The Evening Post would have gone out of
business.
   Now that it's over, I've been
thinking, heck, Letters to the Editor is
for me too, right? Why not tell my side
of the story?
   I'll start with something that will
probably surprise you. What I *really*
wanted in junior high was to be a
cheerleader. If I had made it, all this
would have never happened. . . .

Chapter One

I COULDN'T BELIEVE IT.

I kept staring at the list of names posted outside Miss Strickland's office. The more I stared the more I couldn't believe it.

Other girls came, looked, went. Nobody said anything.

I charged into Miss Strickland's office. She was gone. I ran to the parking lot. There she was, getting into her car, fleeing.

I raced over. She started to pull away. She pretended not to see me. I caught up and knocked on the window. She jerked to a stop, her eyes all wide and innocent. The window came down. She actually smiled.

"Maisie?"

"Miss Strickland . . ." I had to stop and catch my breath. "Miss Strickland, my name's not on the list."

The wide eyes gawked at me. They blinked. "Well, there are quite a few names not on the list."

"Well, yeah," I said, "but that's not . . . I mean . . . there was a mistake. Wasn't there? Shouldn't my name be on it?"

More gawking. The smile looking more and more fake. "I went over the list more than once, but yes, a mistake is always possible. I'll check it again in the morning."

I kept staring, letting her know I wasn't going anywhere. Her smile sagged and finally disappeared. "Maisie, I can't honestly say it's going to make a difference. I have to tell you, you're not going to find your name on the list tomorrow either."

"You mean I *didn't* make cheerleading? Is that what you're saying?"

"I'm sorry."

"*You're* sorry? What about *me*?" I stomped away. I stomped back. "How could I not make it? Didn't I smile enough? Did you ever catch me not smiling? Huh?"

She wagged her head. "No, never."

"And look—*look*"—I tossed my books down and went into my handstand—"what about this? I could walk across the gym floor this way. You could invent a whole new cheer just for this."

I saw her upside-down mouth say, "Maisie, I know you're a very talented girl. There's no specific reason. Forty-six girls came out for cheerleading. We had spots for only five."

I got to my feet. "So why couldn't I be one of the five?"

"Well, I shouldn't tell you this, but if it's any consolation, you would have been next in line."

"Oh great. Who voted against me?" I knew that the already-in cheerleaders helped Miss Strickland pick the new ones.

"No fair," she said. "Maisie, I have to be going. I'm due somewhere in ten minutes. See you tomorrow."

She pulled away.

I called after her. "It was Liz Lampley, wasn't it? *Wasn't* it?"

The car turned onto the street. The window went up.

When I broke the news at dinner that night, all my mother said was "I see," and "Those are the biscuits you like. Buttermilk. Use them to mop up your gravy."

"Do you believe it?" I said.

She shrugged. "I believe everything."

"Oh, that's nice." I served myself some beef stew. "My own mother *expected* me to get cut. Thanks for all the confidence."

She smiled. "I wouldn't have been surprised if you had made it, either."

"So why *didn't* I make it?"

John, my older brother, snorted. "That's easy—you're ugly."

I threw my biscuit at him. P.K., my little sister, howled and threw her biscuit at him. My father slammed his fork on the table. "Another biscuit flies, bodies fly."

John had a biscuit in each hand. "That ain't fair," he whined. "I got a right to get back."

"You called your older sister a name, she got you back with a biscuit. That's fair." My father doesn't care too much if we fight as long as things stay fair.

John jabbed his biscuit at P.K. "I didn't call *her* nothing."

My father finished chewing. "Fine," he said, "call her something."

P.K. shrieked, "Dad-deeeee!"

"Quiet," said my father. "Take it like a man."

"Daddy—I'm *not* a man!"

"Quiet."

The dining room was silent as John thought of a name. Finally an

THERE'S A GIRL IN MY HAMMERLOCK

evil smirk slithered onto his lips. He leaned across the table and sneered: "Watermelon ears."

P.K.'s hands shot to her ears. They're perfectly normal, but some little jerk in nursery school once told her they were big, and she's believed it ever since.

P.K. nailed her eyes to my father. They glazed over. Her lower lip quivered.

Dad whispered, "Hang in there. You can do it."

The lip quivered some more, then settled down. The hands came off the ears. A tear rolled down her cheek, but it bumped into a grin.

My father nodded. "Good."

P.K. beamed proudly and stuck her tongue out at John.

Later, it was just the girls—Mom, P.K., and me—in my room.

"He's right, isn't he?" I said. "I'm ugly."

My mother hoisted P.K. onto her lap. "Now, where have I been? After all this time, I find out I have an ugly child."

P.K. looked up at my mother. "Will I be ugly too when I'm old as Maisie?"

Mom patted her head. "Ugly as a warthog."

"Maybe it's because I don't wear makeup," I said. "And my hair's not long enough. I'm not exactly the Liz Lampley type, you know."

Mom started braiding P.K.'s hair. "What I don't know is why you didn't go out for field hockey like you did last year. I thought you enjoyed it."

"I did. But it's time to move on. You don't want me to stagmate, do you?"

"Stag-nate."

"Whatever. Mom, I'm already in eighth grade. Did you know that your first year as a baby tells what you're gonna be the rest of your life?"

She snapped her fingers. "Then that settles it. You're going to be a bawling, red-faced pooper forever."

P.K. howled. I threw my pillow at her. "Mom, you're not funny. Cheerleaders become somebody. Almost every great woman was a cheerleader once."

"I wasn't."

"You don't count. Mom, listen, here's what I'm gonna do. I'll get up early tomorrow morning, and you can make up my face, you know, really good, eye shadow, blush, the works. Then I'll go into Miss Strickland's and she'll get a load of me and go 'Whoa, what have we here? Maybe we can find room for one more cheerleader.' "

I stared. I waited. "Well?"

"Get me a rubber band."

I got her a rubber band. She tied off the end of P.K.'s pigtail. She pulled the pigtail around and dusted P.K.'s nose with it. P.K. giggled.

I screeched. "Mo-om!"

She looked straight at me. "I wouldn't want you to lower yourself like that."

"Great. Then I'm branded forever. Maisie Potter. Cut from cheerleading. Cut from life."

"Try out next year."

"Next year's too late. My future will be set. I can feel it hardening already." She stood up. "Where are you going?"

"Oh, just down the hallway."

"But we're not done. You gotta help me."

She lowered P.K. to the floor.

"What will help you, young lady, is a good night's sleep."

"Mom, I'm at the crossroads of my life."

She looked at me funny. "Is there something you're not telling me?"

I stared at her. "Huh? What do you mean?"

She smiled. "Oh, nothing." She kissed me.

" 'Night, sweetie."

She led P.K. from my room.

I closed the door.

P.K. was whispering, "What isn't she telling you, Mom?"

Chapter Two

OF COURSE I wasn't telling her something. Of course there was another reason why I was so mad about not making cheerleading. Of course my mother knew it. Of course I hated her.

But I didn't hate Eric Delong.

I used to, the way I hated every other boy in the world. Until the last day at the swim club last summer.

I was playing with my best friend Holly Gish. Underwater hide-and-seek, our own invention. The second time I was It, I opened my eyes underwater and couldn't find her anywhere. I was just about out of breath when I quick-turned, and there was this pair of feet gliding past my nose. I didn't think, I just grabbed the ankle. The ankle shook and flailed. It was definitely not Holly Gish's ankle. It was not any girl's. I let it go. It kicked me in the stomach.

I surfaced. He surfaced.

He was Eric Delong.

We stood there in shoulder-high water, dripping, squinting in the sun.

"Sorry," I said.

He smiled. "That's okay. Did I kick you?"

"Me? No, not me."

"Okay. Seeya."

He swam off.

I guess I went back to playing with Holly. I guess sooner or later I got out of the pool and dried off and changed and went home and had dinner and went to bed and woke up the next morning. I guess the earth kept turning. I guess—because the only thing I'm sure of is that I kept seeing Eric Delong's face in front of me, dripping and water-sparkling and smiling. *That's okay. Did I kick you?* For days, nothing else was real. Holly never called, the sun never went down, he never swam away. *That's okay . . . That's okay . . . That's okay . . .*

What was happening?

I had seen Eric Delong at the pool practically every day during the summer. He was a year ahead of me, going into ninth grade. Big-shot jock. But he had never meant any more to me than a maggot. Like any other boy. Until now.

First day back at school, there I was, craning past the mob in the hallways, trying to catch a glimpse of him. When I finally did see him, and he said "Hi," I almost passed out.

Classes? Subjects? Forget it. The capital of Canada is Eric Delong. Twelve times twelve equals Eric Delong. The action word in a sentence is called Eric Delong.

I'm not totally stupid. I figured out what was going on. I knew what was wrong with me, so to speak. I just never figured it would happen so soon.

I also never figured it would be so complicated. I mean, what was I supposed to do with my whole past life? What about my reputation, thirteen years as one of Lenape Valley's biggest boy-haters? I couldn't tell Holly. I couldn't tell my mother. I couldn't even tell myself.

But feelings, they don't care about telling. They just go right on, piling on top of one another like a big sandwich. I even had feelings about my feelings. One minute I'd be embarrassed, ashamed of myself, a traitor. I spit on the feelings. I hated them. And the next minute I was swimming in them, plunging deep into them, like they were water all warm and sparkly in the pool.

And then, on the second full day of classes, I came out of homeroom and there he was, drinking at the water fountain across the hall.

"Hi, Eric," I called.

He straightened up. He turned. He just had time to say "Hi" back when another "Hi, Eric" came from up the hallway.

Eric turned from me to the other voice. It was Liz Lampley, God's gift to herself. She was heading straight for Eric but her eyes were dead on me. And they knew. Don't ask me how, but they *knew*. Sure enough, coming out of lunch, Luscious Liz slunk up to me. She smiled her rattlesnake smile.

"I didn't know you like him too."

"Like?" I said. "Who?"

"Eric, who else?"

"Eric who?"

She snickered. "Potter, the water fountain. After homeroom."

"I said hello. I'm not allowed to say hello?"

"Not *that* way," she sang.

We were passing a girls' room. I herded her inside with my shoulder and backed her up against the nearest stall door. "You got a problem with how I say hello?" I flattened her nose with my finger. "Huh?"

She gasped. Her eyelids fluttered. She squeaked, "Hey, this isn't Rambo!"

"No?" I said. "Then get outta my face." I spun and walked away.

Her voice stopped me at the door. "Going out for field hockey again this year?"

I turned. She was grinning again. "What's it to you?"

She shrugged. "Oh . . . just thinking. It's too bad we don't cheer for hockey like we do for football."

"Yeah, too bad. I'll really miss you leading all those cheers for me."

She hugged her books to her balloony bosom.

"You know, we stand right behind the *football* team during games. Cheerleaders really get close to the *football* players."

We just stared at each other. Suddenly, I took a quick step forward. She yipped and flinched back. I laughed and opened the door.

"They're switching Eric to quarterback this year, you know," she called. "Because he makes such great passes."

That day, after school, was the first day of tryouts for cheerleading. I was there.

Chapter Three

MY MOTHER WAS RIGHT. A good night's sleep did the trick. Well, maybe nine or ten nights. Anyway, I became myself again.

I was a week late, but the hockey coach let me on the team. We won seven and only lost three. I scored eighteen goals. It was a good season.

The football team only won two games. Well, what could you expect with Lizard Liz leading the cheers? Of course, I never saw them play. We always had a hockey game at the same time, or practice.

Even today, I shudder to think how close I came, me in one of those cutesy blue and gold cheerleader outfits, la-dee-dah. Rah! Rah! Go team! Block that kick! Prancing up and down the sidelines. Gimme an L! Gimme an E! Gimme . . . Gimme a break.

Instead of: Out on the field, playing, not yapping. Moving down the right side, the ball on my stick, cut to the middle, fake feed, freeze the halfback, juke the fullback, wind up—*bam!* Laser beam to the upper left corner of the net. *Potter goal!*

Whew. Goose bumps.

Looking back on early September, I couldn't figure what had gotten into me. Maybe there was something funny in the pool water that day and I swallowed some.

Maybe somebody put a hex on me.

Maybe it was my hormones. I had heard about the teenager gland, the one that dumps a load of hormones into your body and poof! All of a sudden you want to chase boys and have babies and subscribe to *Modern Bride*. Personally, I would never have believed it, but I had seen it happen, so I guessed it was true.

My theory was, maybe my gland opened up that last day in the pool just for a split second, just enough to let one little hormone out. Maybe it was a mistake, like when there's a warm spell in February and the buds are fooled into thinking it's spring.

Or maybe it was on purpose. Maybe it was a scout hormone, sent to check me out, see if I was ready. So it cruises around and goes back and reports to the gland: "Hey, no way, this girl's not ready yet. Go back to sleep." Not even caring how it messed up my life for a week.

Well, if nothing else, it taught me a lesson. Maybe that's what you need now and then, a scare to let you appreciate how good you have it. I had liked my world in those thirteen years before the last day at the swimming pool, and I was glad to be back there.

That's why it didn't bother me that the cheerleader caught the quarterback.

That's why I was nice as pie whenever I saw them together. Which happened a lot once football was over.

Like when I saw the two of them after school one day, in front of his locker. I said hi and they said hi. I even stopped to chitchat for a minute.

When Lizard faked a smile and said, "Going out for basketball again this year?" I didn't say, "What's it to you?" I just smiled back and said, "I guess so."

And when she said, "Oh, I can't *wait* till wrestling season starts," I just smiled some more.

And when she poked him and grinned and said, "I *love* those wrestling suits, they're so *sexy*," I merely smiled even more and said, "Seeya," and bopped on down the hallway. So nice, I could hardly believe myself.

Hey, why not?

I was over him.

Wasn't I?

I didn't care if Liz Lampley snuggled up to him every time I bumped into them. Or if she kept spouting how good he was going to look in his wrestling suit. Or if she kept rubbing my face in it.

Did I?

And even if I did care, there wasn't anything I could do about it.

Was there?

Chapter Four

W*HAT AM I DOING HERE?*

That's what I kept asking myself as I sat in the front row of room 116 after school.

I was the first one there. The others came in. Some by themselves, quiet; others in twos and threes, loud, joking. Until they noticed me. I could hear them sliding into seats. I could feel them staring. I could feel them whispering.

I kept my eyes on the desktop, but the instant *he* came in, I knew. And then *he* was behind me, somewhere. The room was filling up.

The coach came in, Mr. Cappelli. He teaches Health. I didn't have him in class. He didn't seem to notice me. He breezed in and started talking. No, first he wrote something on the blackboard, big letters:

IT TAKES A LITTLE MORE
TO BE A CHAMPION

Then he said, "Gentlemen, welcome to wrestling."

He said a bunch of other stuff, mostly abut Lanape Valley Junior High's great tradition in wrestling, and how we didn't do so hot last year, but "this year we're gonna kick butt and take names." He handed out papers with the tryout schedule and said physical exams would be tomorrow. We all signed a sheet of paper that came around.

End of meeting.

After dinner, brother John came storming into my room. He slammed the door shut. He snarled, "What do you think you're doing?"

"My homework," I said. "Get out."

He picked up Sidney, my furry green snake. "Kruko just called me. I know what you did. You're not funny."

Mike Kruko, our star wrestler.

"Who says I'm trying to be? Put my snake down."

He shook it at me. "I'll wrap it around your skinny neck, girl. You just get your butt over to girls' basketball, where you belong."

I snatched the snake from him. I flogged him in the face with it. He lurched backward. "Don't tell me what to do. And don't tell me where I belong. It's none of your business."

He sneered. "Yeah? Well, maybe it's Mom and Dad's business. Maybe you want to go tell them, huh?" He touched the doorknob. "Maybe you want me to tell them."

I called his bluff. "Go ahead. Don't slam the door on your way out."

He was at my desk before I could turn back to my homework. "I'm telling you, girl, the joke is over. *Don't* show up tomorrow."

I could have jammed my pencil up his nose. I could have ignored him. But what I did was laugh. "Why do you care, anyway?"

He gaped at me while the question sank in. "If you don't know—"

"No," I said, "I *don't* know."

He backed off. "You know what I'm talking about."

I chuckled. "You just don't want anybody to know I'm your sister, that's all."

"*Sister?* Sisters don't go out for wrestling. It looks like I had a brother all these years and didn't even know it."

"Does that mean I can leave the toilet seat up all the time like you do?"

He flashed into my face. "I'm just telling you—" He glared. I glared. He went to the door, yanked it open, jabbed his finger at me, and stomped off with his last word: "*Don't.*"

I did.

Chapter Five

WE WAITED IN THE GYM.

The stands were pulled down on one side. I sat on the top row, at the end. I felt better with the wall behind me. The others sat lower, in a bunch. Mr. Cappelli had said there were fifty-five of us. I wondered if that included me. There were seven empty rows in front of me. I counted them.

On the gym floor, the boys' basketball team was trying out. John was one of them. He kept glaring up at me.

The doctor was in Mr. Cappelli's office. Every five minutes or so, Mr. Cappelli would pop out and call three names. Each time three guys got up and headed for the office, others in the stands would hoot stuff like, "Don't let'm squeeze too hard!" and "When he says cough, give him a kiss!"

Ha ha.

An hour passed. Eric Delong was one of the first to go. The bunch got smaller and smaller, till only four of us were left. Then the others went in.

I waited forever.

Did Mr. Cappelli think I was joking? Had he not even noticed me? Had the doctor gone home? Would I be sitting there all night?

At long last: "Potter!"

I got up. I tripped over the first bleacher and dumped my books all over the place. Howls came from the basketball court. Somehow I got down to the floor without killing myself. I scrambled around under the stands for my books, bonked my head a couple of times, and aimed for the office. By then I was shaking like a seventh-grader in a ninth-grade study hall.

There are actually two offices, an inner one and an outer one. Mr. Cappelli and the doctor were in the outer one, talking and laughing. Mr. Cappelli was sprawled in a tilt-back chair, his feet on the desk. The doctor sat on a corner of the desk. He didn't have a white coat, but he did have a stethoscope dangling from his neck.

The doctor smiled at me when I came in. He looked friendly

enough, but I wished he was a woman doctor, like the one my mom takes me to. He motioned with his arm. "Into my office, Miss Potter."

He waited at the doorway while I went in. He closed the door. The door had a tall glass window with a curtain over it.

He pointed to a chair. "You can put your books there."

I wanted to keep hold of them, but I put them down.

"Okay, now you can sit up here." He patted the desk. I lifted myself onto it.

Suddenly the famous tomahawk-shaped silver hammer was in his hand. He bonked me in the knee with it. My leg jumped. Same with the other leg.

"Good," he said.

He put the hammer down. He stuck the ends of the stethoscope in his ears and put the thing on my chest. He listened for a while. "Should I breathe?" I said. He shook his head no. I thought that answered it, but then I realized I was confused. I had meant, Should I breathe deep? Was he telling me, No, don't breathe deep, or No, don't breathe at all.

Before I had it figured out, he straightened up. "Okay." He moved to the side and put the scope on my back. "Deep breath." Ah, okay. I took a deep breath. He moved the scope to three other spots on my back. I took a deep breath at each one. He didn't have to tell me.

All this time I kept thinking about what doctors do to boys to check for hernias, the feeling, the coughing. One question kept going through my mind: *Do girls get hernias?*

He backed off. "Okay, so far so good. Now, let's have you get down from there."

I got down. I thought: *Uh-oh, here it comes.* I checked the curtain to make sure it was covering the window.

He was behind me.

"I want you to stand straight for me, feet together, look straight ahead." I did. "Okay, now, I'm going to ask you to reach behind and pull up the back of your shirt."

I felt like saying, Well, if you're going to *ask* me, go ahead and *ask* me. But I just did it.

"Higher, please," he said.

I pulled my shirt higher. I could feel goose bumps popping all over my back. My bra was showing.

"And," he cooed, "just a smidgeon higher."

"What's a smidgeon?" I said.

"A little more."

"Up to my *neck?*"

"That would be perfect."

I had to do some fancy contorting, tugging the back of my shirt all the way up while trying to keep my front covered.

"Okay, Miss Potter, now I want you to keep your legs straight and bend forward from the waist. Let's do it slowly. Try to touch your toes."

Oh my God, I thought, *it's worse than they do with boys!*

There I was, my back totally naked, except for my bra, bending over farther and farther, till I was nothing but a rear-end in this guy's face. Fingertips ran down my spine. My goose bumps felt as big as my backbone bumps.

I cringed, waited for the next move.

"Okay," he said.

"Okay what?"

"That's it."

I pulled my shirt down and straightened up. "That's *it?*"

He nodded. "You're fit as a fiddle."

"I can go?"

"Yep."

I got my books. I looked at him. "Are you a doctor?"

His face was blank. Then he broke out laughing. "I hope so." He pulled out his wallet and took a little white card from it. He gave it to me. It said:

David L. Wycoff, M.D.
Family Practice

"I'm in the Yellow Pages." He smiled. He opened the door for me. I didn't look at Mr. Cappelli. I just kept going. But he called me. "Potter."

I stopped, turned. "Yes?"

He reached across the desk, a white envelope in his hand. "This is for your parents." He slipped it into one of my books.

I waited a second, but he didn't say anything else. He wasn't smiling, like the doctor.

I left.

The note said that Mr. Cappelli wanted to meet with me and my parents as soon as possible. He wrote his home phone number for them to call him.

"What's this about?" said my father. "Who's this Vincent Cappelli?"

"Uh, he's a teacher," I said.

"Why's he want to see us?"

"He teaches Health."

"You didn't answer my question."

My father was staring at me. My mother was staring at me. My brother was lurking in the background.

"Maybe he heard how healthy I am. Maybe he's going to be sick and he wants me to substitute teach for him."

John laughed.

"Get outta here!" I yelled.

My mother pointed to the stairs. "John—you have homework."

John went up, still snickering.

My mother turned to me. "Maisie, you're not in trouble, are you?"

"No, Mom, jeez. Just because I got a note?"

She took the note from my father. "Then why did you get this?"

"Mom, I don't know. He didn't tell me. He just said give this to your parents."

"Health teacher."

"Well . . ." I wished I could get out from under her eyes. "I don't know. He's a coach too."

"Coach? Basketball?" For the hundredth time she looked at the note. "Isn't your basketball coach Mrs. Fox?"

I just stared at her for about an hour, like, duhhhhh. Until my father snatched the note from her hand and headed for the phone. That's when I got outta there.

Since there were no explosions in the house the rest of the night, I figured Mr. Cappelli must not have told them exactly what he was the coach of.

Chapter Six

"**W**RESTLING?!"

We were in the principal's office, but you could probably hear my father's roar from Home Ec to Woodshop. Mr. Cappelli had just said it. He gave me a hard look and said to my father, "I guess she didn't tell you."

My father kept staring at me as he spoke. "She just said you were a coach."

They had plunked me in a big red leather chair. I shrank back into it. I wished I could wrap its arms around me.

Mr. Cappelli told them about me coming to the sign-up meeting and the physical exam. "Doing that," he said, "made me think she was serious. So I gave her the note to take home." He looked at me. "You should have told your parents."

I was afraid to try my voice. I just nodded.

"*Wrestling?*" My father kept saying the word, like it was foreign and he wasn't sure what it meant. "I thought you were going to play basketball, like last year."

I stared. I shrugged.

"What's *that* supposed to mean?"

My time was running out. I looked at my mom. I couldn't tell anything from her face. "I don't like basketball," I said.

"You played it," my father said. It sounded like an accusation.

"I don't *want* to play it anymore!" I blurted out. "I want to do something else after school. I like swimming, but they don't have swimming in junior high. So I went out for wrestling. Girls wrestle on TV. What about Washerwoman and Ma Barker? What am I, a criminal?" I pounded the red leather seat cushion, not because I was mad at them, but at myself for crying.

Suddenly my mom was on the arm of the chair, pulling me into her soft sweater.

I heard my father sigh. After a while, he said, not as loud as before, "Is she allowed?"

Mr. Hobbs, the principal, said, "Oh yes." The last time I was this close to Mr. Hobbs was at the final assembly last year, when he gave me the award for Outstanding Seventh Grade Female Athlete. "The law says she's allowed all right, as long as there's no wrestling program for girls. I guess the question is, do *you* say she's allowed?"

I knew what my father wanted to say. But he didn't say it, he just stared at my mother.

Her voice was gentle in my ear. "Do you really want to?"

I nodded.

Her hand squeezed me tighter. My father turned away and looked at the wall.

Mr. Cappelli cleared his throat. "Mr. and Mrs. Potter, the main reason I wanted to meet with you, and have Mr. Hobbs sit in too, was to make sure everybody knows what we're getting into here. To put it bluntly, wrestling is a men and boys' world. Believe me, I know. I've wrestled and coached for almost twenty years now. Legally, she can do it. But there's no law that says she has to be welcome."

I felt my mother stiffen. "Won't she be welcome with you, Mr. Cappelli?"

Mr. Cappelli gave a snorty little chuckle and shook his head. "Okay—here's my position. I've never had a girl try out before. I'd rather not have one. But if she insists, I won't try to stop her. Let me tell you, there are coaches in this league who would. They would make sure she was always paired with somebody thirty pounds heavier. They would find something to holler at her every minute. They wouldn't have to cut her. She would quit."

My mother's voice was quiet and pleasant. "But you wouldn't do that, would you?"

Mr. Cappelli came closer. His beard, even though he shaved, was a million tiny black dots. One white strand stood out in his black hair. "No, I wouldn't," he said. "Once she walks into that wrestling room, as far as I'm concerned, she's the same as everybody else. I stress hard work, discipline, and a team concept. When it comes down to final cut day, I won't care if she's a boy, a girl, or a banana. If it can wrestle and keep its grades up, it's on my team." He looked sideways at me. "As long as it doesn't cry."

My mother nodded. "Fair enough."

Mr. Cappelli glanced at my father. My father wasn't talking.

"Mrs. Potter—Maisie—I have to say this, and I don't mean it to sound sexist or whatever. Boys are strong. They're used to playing rough. I've got"—he chuckled—"I've got some nasty little critters on that team. Hard-as-nails little guys. And *they* get hurt. Understand what I'm saying." He leaned toward me. "*They* get hurt."

My mom sniffed. "Maisie's been hurt before."

"My practices are tough," said Mr. Cappelli. "We practice every school day and through Christmas vacation. I'm known for having the longest and toughest workouts around."

"Maisie wouldn't have it any other way."

The craziest thought flashed through my brain: My mother wants me to wrestle more than I do!

My mother went on: "Mr. Cappelli, maybe Maisie won't even make the team. I can only tell you that if she doesn't, it won't be because she quit. When you talk about boys being stronger, you may be right about arms and legs. But nobody"—she squeezed me—"nobody is as strong in the heart as this little girl right here."

Mr. Cappelli nodded. He half-smiled. He backed off.

Mr. Hobbs cleared his throat. "Vince, the problems don't necessarily end in the wrestling room, do they?"

"No," said Mr. Cappelli. "The wrestling room could be the easiest of it. If she does make the team, you might find yourself wishing she didn't."

"Other students can be harsh," said Mr. Hobbs. "Even parents."

"Okay," said my mother. There was a snap to her voice. "Let's get it settled right now."

Her hand cupped my chin and pulled my face around and up till I was looking at her. "Maisie, do you realize there are differences between boys and girls?"

"Mom!"

She squeezed my chin. "Answer, please."

"Yeah."

"You're in school."

"Yes."

"Do you realize the kinds of situations you could get into? On the mat? Wrestling with a boy?"

"Yes."

"Can you imagine the kinds of things people might think about a girl wrestling with boys?"

"Yes."

"And the kinds of things they might say?"

"Yes."

"Final question. Do you care?"

"No."

"Final, *final* question. No more tears?"

"No."

She winked at me and released my face. She stood up. She spread her hands. She gave everybody a big smile. "There you are."

A minute later I was heading for lunch.

Chapter Seven

FIRST STOP after changing into sweat stuff was the coach's office. That's where the scale was. We had to get weighed before and after each practice.

We waited in line, all fifty-five of us. I stepped up. Mr. Cappelli slid the jiggers. His eyes never left the scale.

"One-oh-five," he said.

Mr. Paul, the assistant coach, wrote it down.

Into the wrestling room. Hanging around till everybody got weighed.

I checked the place out. It was the size of half a basketball court. Three big blue mats were shoved together to make one huge mat covering almost the whole floor.

There was that saying again, on a big banner across one wall:

IT TAKES A LITTLE MORE TO BE A CHAMPION

The walls were full. There were big poster-board charts with headings like "Beast of the Week" and "Fastest Pin" and "Nutcracker." There were newspaper clippings and mottos and team pictures and tons of color snapshots: Lenape Valley wrestlers in action, Lenape Valley wrestlers with medals hanging from their necks, Lenape Valley wrestlers holding trophies. A scrapbook on walls.

A whistle blew. Everybody turned. Mr. Cappelli hollered, "Okay, people, spread out for stretching. Follow Kruko."

Mike Kruko stepped to the front. He was scowling. "Okay, you rookies, watch." He bent down, with his legs straight, and touched the floor in three spots with his fingertips. He straightened up. "Okay, do it. Count, One-two-three-*one* . . . one-two-three-*two* . . ."

No problem. I locked my knees. I touched the mat easy. By five, I was even curling my fingers and touching my knuckles. I hoped the coaches were watching. I checked out the kids around me. Some couldn't even reach down to their toes.

We went to ten on those. Then we did a bunch of other stretching exercises: the waist, the neck, the legs.

I was smokin'.

"Monkey rolls!" Mr. Cappelli called.

He pulled three veterans up front to demonstrate. Three people in a row. You're either rolling on the mat or jumping over somebody who is. Like juggling with your body. It looked like fun.

"Okay," called the coach, "get in threes. Monkey rolls. Do it!"

Within two seconds, I was alone. Everybody else was threed up, doing monkey rolls.

Coach hollered: "Anybody left over, do it yourself! Move!"

So there I was, flopping to the mat, rolling, jumping up. Down-roll-up, down-roll-up. I felt like the world's biggest jerk.

Sit-ups were next. Fifty. No sweat.

Then push-ups. Not just regular push-ups. You had to put your hands together with your thumbs and forefingers forming a diamond shape. "Diamond-ups" the coach called them. We had to do twenty-five. Up till arms straight, down till nose touching. I did eleven the right way. I had to cheat the rest. Now I hoped the coaches weren't watching. When I stood up, I thought spaghetti was hanging from my shoulders.

Next we ran, out in the hallways. First we did four laps around the whole school. Then we went to the long, wide hallway past the lunchroom. We were split into groups of five. We did sprints. The finish line was a water fountain.

Who winds up in my sprint group but Eric Delong. Up till then, I had been too busy to think about him. As we crouched to start, he was right next to me.

I smiled. I said, "Hi." He didn't answer. He didn't even look at me. He just stared down the hallway, all grim and serious. I was wondering if he heard me, or if I should say something else, or if I should kill myself, when Mr. Cappelli shouted "Go!" Eric and the rest took off. I was still five yards behind when they hit the water fountain.

Each group ran twice. I was fuming all the way back to the starting line. I'm not just fast for a girl. I'm fast, period. Unless you were a sprinter on the track team, you probably couldn't beat me.

The other four were lined up for the second race. I pushed my way in beside Delong. "Excuse me," I said. I knew he was gawking at me but I didn't look over. I was off with the "Go!" By the second lunchroom door I was alone. All the way I kept watching Mr. Cappelli watching me. His expression never changed. I breezed past the water fountain. I threw up my hands and clapped. "Yeah!"

Then everybody was jogging in a crowd back to the wrestling room. Suddenly I got slammed in the shoulder. I didn't stop lurching till I hit the wall. The crowd went jogging by.

"Hey!" I yelled.

Nobody turned.

Back in the wrestling room, Mr. Cappelli grouped us into weight classes. Besides me, there were three others in the 105-pound class: a ninth-grader, another eighth-grader, and a seventh-grader.

The first thing Mr. Cappelli showed us was the stance for when you start a bout. How to hold your arms, crouch, bend your knees, shuffle, don't cross-step, keep your balance, rear end back, rear end low, head up, circle, circle. Oh yeah, scowl. Nobody said so, but scowling seemed to be a big part of wrestling.

I did my stance with Burke, the other eighth-grader. I circled, shuffled, kept my rear end down. The kid's scowl stunk. Mine beat his by a mile. I hoped the coach caught it.

Next we learned the referee's position. In my group I started as the down person. That meant I got on my hands and knees, like a floor-scrubber.

Nobody wanted to be my up person. The ninth-grader told Burke to do it. Burke told the seventh-grader. The seventh-grader looked like he was going to faint.

He knelt on one knee, like Mr. Cappelli showed us, sort of beside and over me. One hand grabbed my elbow—well, more grazed than grabbed. His other arm curled around my waist, his hand on my stomach. He was shaking.

I giggled. I couldn't help it. I pushed his hand away. He put it back. I giggled louder.

The coach thundered: "Potter!"

"Yes, sir?"

The seventh-grader vanished.

"What's so funny?"

"Nothing."

"One more chance, Potter. What's so funny?"

I gulped. I cleared my throat. "It—uh—tickled."

I could sense fifty-four laugh bombs being swallowed.

"Potter."

"Yes, sir?"

I stood up.

"Give me five fast laps around the school, Potter. After each lap, do five push-ups. Next time you laugh will be the last time. You got it?"

"Yes, sir."

"Move!"

I moved.

"Potter!" he called as I headed down the hallway. "If you feel like running right on home, nobody's gonna stop you!"

Nothing like feeling wanted.

I did my laps. I did my push-ups. I got funny looks from teachers. I cursed my ticklish stomach. I could still feel the kid's arm around my waist. No boy ever did that before. It was the closest I ever came to dancing. (Not counting the time with my uncle Harry at my cousin Maureen's wedding.) It was weird. I didn't much like it. Would I have liked it if the arm had belonged to Eric Delong?

I thought I saw a little surprise on the coach's face when I got back to the wrestling room. The others were leaving. He made me stay and do more push-ups, more sit-ups, more one-person monkey rolls.

I could barely stand on the scale afterward. I now weighed 103. In the locker room I lost some more. I threw up.

Chapter Eight

I KNEW MY MOTHER was out there somewhere. I could recognize her voice.

"Maisie, wake up. It's after seven."

"Morning or night?"

"Open your eyes."

"I can't. They hurt."

Fingers pried my eyelids apart. A face appeared. Green. Fuzzy. Silly mouthed. Red tongue. Bulging eyes . . . *Mom?*

No . . . Sidney, my snake.

Two fingers pinched my nose, swiveled my head. *There* she was.

"I would think you'd had enough sleep," she said. She pulled me to a sitting position. "Look at you."

I looked.

"You're dressed. You slept in your clothes."

She was right.

"Dragging in last night looking like a zombie. Not eating your dinner."

"I didn't?"

"You fell asleep right at the table."

"I did?"

"Only thing out of your mouth was some mumbling about push-ups."

I flopped down. "Don't say that word."

She pulled me up. "You crawled upstairs and that was the last anybody saw of you. Did you have homework?"

"What's homework?"

She gave her prime-time sigh of disgust. She yanked the covers off my legs. "You didn't even take your *shoes* off!" She pulled them off for me. And my socks. "Now get changed."

"I can't," I groaned. "I can't mooooove."

"Did you think wrestling was going to be easy? Stop being a baby."

"Just let me stay in bed and be a baby today. I'll be big again tomorrow." I flopped back down.

She yanked me clear out of the bed and onto my feet. "Get. Dressed."

I tried to lift my arms to take my shirt off. "They won't go up!"

She grabbed my face. "*You* are going to school if I have to carry you."

She undressed me. I couldn't remember the last time my mother did that. I didn't care. She took my old stuff off and put new stuff on.

"You got some phone calls last night," she said. "I know one of them was Holly."

I groaned. "The poop is hitting the fan."

"Fine," she said. "Take an umbrella. Now go to the bathroom." She pushed me off.

Every move I made, something new ached. My toes ached. My teeth ached. I went into the bathroom. I sat down . . .

Next thing I knew, my mother was shaking me awake. "I don't believe you." She ran water and mopped my face with a cold washcloth. She stuck it down my back. I screamed. "Now, stay awake," she commanded.

I was going to be late. Not that I cared, but my mother did. She rammed some breakfast down my throat and drove me to school.

Outside was deserted. I was still in the hallway when last bell rang. I ran. I was surprised that I could. I barged into homeroom. Every head jerked up. Only because I'm late? I wondered.

Holly nabbed me on the way to first period math. Her eyes practically devoured my face. "Is it true?"

"Is what true?" I said.

"You're out for *wrestling?*"

"Guess so."

"*Boys'* wrestling?"

"There's *girls'* wrestling?"

She pulled me out of the flow, against the lockers. She growled. "Maisie, are you crazy? Do you know what people are saying?"

I looked her in the eye. "What are *you* saying, Holly?"

She sneered. "Hah! Know what I'm saying? I'm saying how come I had to hear about it from fifty *other* people? How come my best friend didn't tell me *herself?* How come I gotta feel like a *jerk?*"

"I'm sorry," I said. "From now on, every time I do something, I'll get your permission so you won't feel like a jerk."

She glared. I glared. She stomped off.

She didn't speak to me again till third period English.

"Maisie, we need you for girls' basketball. You'd be a star."

"Why should I want to be a star?"

"Why *shouldn't* you?"

"Why *should* I?"

We were practically screaming.

I stared at her. "Holly . . . why do you *care*? Huh?"

She just stood there, like my brother when I asked him the same thing. Her eyes were wide and wet. Finally she squeaked, "I *don't*," and stomped off again.

Sure enough, next period she was in my face again. This time she looked different, grimmer. "I don't believe you," she snarled.

She dragged me into an empty classroom and slammed the door shut. Then she shoved me up against the blackboard.

This wasn't like Holly. She's pretty meek, not the physical type. There was nobody else I would let do that to me.

She shoved me again. "You jerk."

"Don't press your luck," I told her.

She sneered. "I found out your little secret."

"Is that so?" I said. "Want to tell me about it? I didn't know I had one."

She shoved me aside, snatched a piece of chalk, and wrote in huge letters, taking up the whole blackboard:

ERIC DELONG

She slammed down the chalk. "Does that name happen to ring a bell?"

I just gaped at the blackboard.

"Your good buddy Liz Lampley told me. By now she's probably told the whole school."

She backed off. Now she was inspecting me, her mouth twisting like she had just found me crawling up her pantleg. "God, Maisie, chasing him onto the *wrestling* team? Are you that hard up?"

This time it was me who stomped off.

Chapter Nine

THE NOTE WAS WAITING FOR ME after school, sticking out of the door slit of my locker. I opened it. It started: "If you think by going out for wrestling you can get Eric away from me . . ." I didn't bother to finish it. I ripped it up and trashed it on my way to practice.

Four people had dropped out of tryouts. We were now down to fifty-one.

Somehow I had lost another pound. "One-oh-two," Mr. Cappelli called at the scale.

One thing there wasn't less of was pain. I hurt so much. Not only couldn't I touch the mat, I could hardly touch my knees. I finally made it down to my shoe tops.

Diamond-ups? I did two right. The rest were gruesome.

That's how it went with the rest of the exercises. Somehow I got through them, but just to do them wrong I had to kill myself.

At least this time I had two partners to do monkey rolls with: Bamberger, the seventh grade 105-pounder, and a 70-pounder, the littlest kid in the place. I wasn't about to do it alone again. As soon as Mr. Cappelli yelled "Monkey rolls!" I grabbed them and said, "You're with me." They didn't argue.

Eric Delong didn't race me in the hallway sprints this time, but I still won. The laps around the school were another story. We were packed pretty tight. I was in the middle, jogging along, when a foot behind me clipped my heels. I lurched, clawed at the sweatshirt in front of me, and went down, flat on my face in front of the library. Sneakers and snickers hurdled me. The pack ran on. The librarian came out and gave me a dirty look.

I wanted to keep running right on home.

Back in the wrestling room, we paired off for the stance. I grabbed Bamberger, the 105-pound seventh-grader. I was starting to feel comfortable with him. Plus, I could boss him. He was timid, even for a seventh-grader.

I asked him what his first name was.

"George," he said.

George Bamberger. His name didn't seem to fit. Too heavy. His voice was almost as high as a girl's.

"I'm Maisie."

"I know," he said.

"Stance!" called Mr. Cappelli. "Butt low, head up, don't cross-step, shuffle, shuffle, circle, circle."

We lowered our butts. We lifted our heads. We shuffled, shuffled, circled, circled.

George's eyes darted around. He whispered, "You okay?"

I stopped. I stared at him.

"Potter, move!" came the coach's holler.

I moved. "Yeah," I whispered, "I'm okay."

George gave a little smile. It looked like I had at least one friend on the team.

Mr. Cappelli was booming: "Stance or dance, you two!"

We jammed our butts down and out, shuffled, circled.

"Want to dance?" I whispered.

He giggled.

"No giggling," I warned him. "You're a wrestler. Scowl."

We scowled as we shuffled and circled, fiercer and fiercer. I bared my teeth. He flared his nostrils. I hissed. He snarled. I snorted. Pretty soon we were circling like a pair of chimps, arms hanging down, going, "ou-ou, ou-ou."

And Mr. Cappelli was going, "Potter! Bamberger! Five laps, twenty push-ups, and into my office."

We did our laps and push-ups and went to the office.

"I'm sorry I got you into trouble," I said.

He shrugged. I felt rotten.

Mr. Cappelli didn't come in till practice was over. He slammed the door. His eyes drove a stake through me.

He stood over me, hands on hips. "What kind of game are you playing?"

How was I supposed to answer that?

"Why are you doing this?"

I stared up at him.

He gave a funny-sounding snort and wagged his head. He sat on the edge of his desk. The thing on his face was almost a smile. His voice was almost friendly. "You don't *really* want to be out for wrestling, do you?"

I was going to answer but he went on. "This is a joke, right? A prank. Somebody put you up to it. A couple of your friends? Maybe it was a bet? Potter stays out for wrestling for a week, she wins. Right?"

"There's no bet," I told him.

"You don't have to watch what you say now. There are no parents in here, no principal."

I repeated, "There's no bet."

The coach rolled his eyes to the ceiling. He took a deep breath. He turned to Bamberger.

"And you. I thought you wanted to be a wrestler."

George was scared stiff. He just nodded.

I spoke up. "It's really not his fault, Coach. I was making him laugh."

The coach practically pounced on me. His finger quivered an inch from my nose. "*You* shut up. *I'll* decide who's at fault around here. You understand?"

"Yes, sir."

"You under*stand?*"

"Yes, sir!"

He turned back to George. "Bamberger, if you want to have a prayer of making this team, you'll come in with a new attitude tomorrow. Understand?"

George gulped. "Yes, sir."

"And that means paying attention to me and *not* to this"—he flung a finger at me—"this dipstick. Now get outta here."

Bamberger got out.

Mr. Cappelli re-shut the door. He walked around the desk a couple of times. He started talking in a low, almost nice voice. That's what fooled me, because the tone of the voice didn't fit the words.

"It's coming clearer to me every day now. You're a fake. You're a troublemaker. My guess is you're a glutton for attention. You want to be a freak sideshow—the girl who wrestles boys."

I couldn't believe it. I was still steaming from "dipstick" and now he was laying all this other crap on me, my own coach.

"Step right up, ladies and gentlemen. Get your ticket. You won't believe your eyes. You heard of the bearded lady? The eight-hundred-pound man? The geek who bites the heads off chickens? Well, you ain't seen nothin' yet, folks. Not till you've seen the little lady who wrestles boys on the mat. Big boys. Little boys. She grapples. She scrapples. Step right up, folks. You ain't seen a freak till you've seen the grappling girlie—"

I stood up. "Are you through?"

He pointed to the chair. "Sit down."

"No," I said.

I thought he would kill me. Instead, he laughed. "Fine. Suit yourself."

His face got serious. "Just between you and me, Potter, if I thought I could get away with it, you'd be out of here now. Even so, your days are numbered. State law or no state law, this is my team. I'll pick my people."

He smiled. He actually looked friendly. "Look, the weekend's coming up. Go home. Get back with your family and friends. Where you belong. Where you really want to be. Monday comes"—he walked to the door, opened it, smiling—"be over on the girls' basketball court. Not here."

I walked out.

The girls' basketball team was in the locker room. I could hear one shower running. The rest was silence and underwear. Everybody busy getting dressed, showing me their backsides, not their faces.

Holly was at her locker. She knew I was there. She didn't turn.

The shower stopped and suddenly it wasn't silent anymore.

"Yo, Potter!"

Out of the shower came Tall Tina McIntire, starting center, wet, gleaming, brown, all six feet of her. Standing there naked, the towel just hanging from her hand, like she was daring everyone to stare at her.

"What do you think, Maypot?" she called, looking around. "These people stink or what?" She pinched her nose. "Oo-wee!"

I couldn't help chuckling. Most of the girl jocks in our school would rather put their clothes on over a gallon of practice sweat than expose themselves in the shower.

She dripped on over to me. She palmed my head. Her fingers were so long she could have picked both my ears at once.

"I can't believe you're deserting me," she said.

I shrugged. "You'll do okay."

"Okay?" she squawked. "You kidding? Who's gonna bring the ball up? Who's gonna pop the outside shot? And most important of all—who's gonna work it into me?" She flung her hand. "*These* clowns?"

Typical Tina. Blaring out the truth but making it funny, hard to get mad at.

I re-shrugged.

She hoisted a foot onto the bench and dried it. Everybody else I've ever seen starts drying from the top down. Leaning over brought her face down to my level. She grinned. "We had it going last year, didn't we, Maypot?"

I grinned. I nodded. "Yeah."

"We did it, didn't we, girl?"

I pictured us the year before. Me and Tina. Mutt and Jeff. Tearing it up.

I heard Mr. Cappelli's voice: *Be over on the basketball court. Not here . . . Not here . . .*

"Yeah," I said, "we sure did."

Chapter Ten

I'M QUITTING," I told my mother after dinner.

"Quitting what?"

"What do you think? Wrestling."

"Fine."

"Did you hear me? I said I'm quitting."

"I said fine."

We were in the bathroom. My mother was replacing the old shower head, which no longer showered you, it attacked you. It thought it was a water cannon.

"Why isn't Daddy doing that?" I asked her.

"He's doing something else."

"So? Tell him."

"Why?"

She was straddling the tub, working a pair of pliers. "You're going to fall," I told her.

"You'll catch me." She grunted. "This isn't budging." She handed me the pliers. "Pass me the monkey wrench."

The tools were on the toilet seat.

"Which one's the monkey wrench?"

"The one that looks like a monkey."

"Hilarious, Mom." I gave her the thing that wasn't a screwdriver or a hammer. "So what do you think about me quitting?"

"I think it's your decision."

"Aren't you going to try to talk me out of it?"

"Nope." She grunted. "Ah—it's moving."

"But you *are* disappointed, right?"

"No. Actually, I'm quite happy with this wrench. *There* . . ." She held out the old shower head proudly. "It's off."

"Congratulations. I know what you're thinking. You said I wouldn't quit, and here I am quitting. You're thinking, Boy, did I have this kid figured out wrong." I looked up at her. "Right?"

Her answer was a chuckle. She gave me the old shower head. "Pass me the thread sealer."

I looked around. "Huh?"

"The white tapelike stuff."

I gave it to her. She unwound some and started wrapping it around the threads of the headless shower pipe. I was slightly amazed. "You actually know what you're doing?"

"Incredible, isn't it?"

"Don't you even want to know why I'm quitting?"

She cut the tape and pressed it into the threads. "Of course I do."

"Well, it's because it's not what it was supposed to be. I've been out wrestling for two days now and we did everything but wrestle."

"That so? Pass me the new shower head."

I passed it to her. "Yeah. We run. We do monkey rolls, push-ups, exercises. We scowl. We circle. We stick our butts out."

"Sounds like fun to me. Speaking of monkeys, give me the wrench again."

"Yeah, fun all right . . . here . . . I tried to have fun, know what it got me? Five laps and twenty push-ups."

"So you're quitting."

"Mom, everybody hates me. The other wrestlers hate me. My old basketball team ignores me except for Tina. The whole school's talking about me."

"I thought you said"—she stopped to grunt and do some serious wrenching—"you didn't care."

"I never thought even Holly would hate me." I was afraid to tell her the biggest reason of all: the rotten things the coach had said, that he practically ordered me to never come back.

When my mother said "Holly hates you?" it was more to the shower than to me. She gave a final wrench and grunt. "Nnnnn-*uh*. There." She stepped down from the tub. "Say a prayer it works."

She gave me a brave smile, took a deep breath, counted, "One—two—*three*—" and turned on the faucet.

It worked!

A cone-shaped shower of water fell from the head to the tub.

I held out my hand. She slapped it. "We did it!"

"You did it, Mom," I said. "Way to go."

Almost every Friday night, Holly and I slept over. One week her house, next week mine. Sometimes we'd set it up at school, sometimes over the phone. But most times we'd just show up at each other's front door after dinner that night. That was almost my favorite part, that we didn't have to plan it.

This week it was her turn to sleep over at my house. It was already seven-thirty.

I knew what she was up to. She was waiting for me to call, say I was sorry or something like that.

By eight o'clock I had decided two things: one, I would not call her; two, I would not tell her I was quitting. Why give her the satisfaction?

The phone rang. I ran to answer. It wasn't her. It was a man's voice, gruff, asking for my father. "Tell him to call me when he gets in," said Mr. Gruff. He left his number, no name, and hung up.

When my father got home, I gave him the message. He called. I hung around.

At first my father was stony, saying, "Yeah . . . yeah . . ." Then he was saying more, like, "That's your problem" and "It's up to her." Then he was mad. "Listen, eightball, you raise your kid, I'll raise mine." He hung up.

"What was that all about?" I said.

He stared at me. He wagged his head. He smirked. "Some eight-ball. Father of one of the wrestlers."

"Who?"

"Zales, I think he said."

Bobby Zales was a 115-pounder. Eighth-grader.

"So what did he want?"

My father snorted. "You. Off the team."

"Huh?"

I followed him into the kitchen. He got the ice cream and scooped out a cereal-bowl-full of heavenly hash for himself.

"That's too much junk," I told him.

He jabbed his spoon at me. "Hey, don't *you* start."

"So what do you mean," I said, "me off the team?"

"He said if you stay on the team, he's pulling his kid off."

"So what did you say?"

"I said fine, pull him off."

"Well," I said, "you should've told him no problem. Because I'm quitting." He just stared at me.

"What're you looking mad for?" I said. "You never wanted me to wrestle anyway. You're getting your wish."

He stared. He said, "You're not quitting."

"Really?" I said. "How come all of a sudden you're changing your tune?"

He sucked a spoonful of ice cream. "I'm against some eightball trying to tell my kid what to do."

Something warm puffed inside me. I felt good.

But I didn't want to feel good.

"I'll quit if I want," I said, and walked away.

I went to my room. I wanted to be alone. So naturally, in waltzes P.K. with her bunny pajamas and hippopotamus slippers, all cheery.

She bounced on my bed, holding a new poster in front of her. It was so big, it blotted her out. It was Washerwoman, the TV wrestler. It showed her with her pail of soapy water and her sponge and mop, looking nasty and itching to clean up her next victim.

Washerwoman was our hero. We watched her on Saturday mornings. Her archenemy was Ma Barker, with her cigar and machine gun. We hated Ma Barker.

P.K. pulled the top edge of the poster down to her chin. "Mommy got it today. It's mine. It's not yours."

"Off the bed," I told her.

She bounced off. She lifted a foot. "See? Hippotatapuss."

I didn't answer. I didn't look.

"Wanna rassle, Maisie?" She grabbed my leg.

I shook her off. "No."

"Did you rassle Washerwoman yet, Maisie? Huh? Didja body-slam her?"

I jumped in her face. "It's *wrestle*. You got it? *Wrestle*. Not *rassle*, dummy."

She gaped at me. Her lower lip came out like a plum. She bolted from the room.

"Thanks for shutting the door!" I called. I slammed it shut myself.

I whipped some clothes against the wall. I ripped some paper. I snapped a pencil in half. I booted my sneakers. One sailed high enough to knock my framed Outstanding Seventh Grade Female Athlete certificate off the wall. It crashed down like World War Three.

Outside I heard my mother say to somebody, "Leave her alone."

Right, I sneered, don't go near the monster. That suited me fine. I turned out my light and flopped onto my bed.

You would have thought I'd feel better, deciding to quit. All I felt was rottener. And confused. I wanted to cry, scream, and laugh all at once.

Why was I doing this to myself?

Why couldn't I just be a nice, normal girl? Why didn't I giggle and wiggle more? Holly said I could have one of the best wiggles in school, if only I'd work on it a little.

Why didn't I throw or run like Liz Lampley? Little mincey, cutesy, dainty, peetee steps: *peetee-peetee-peetee-peetee*.

Why didn't I wear lipstick? Or earrings? God, what kind of girl *was* I? Thirteen years old and my ears not pierced. Babies were ahead of me.

And most of all, why—*why*—did I ever go out for wrestling?

In my head, I listed the possible reasons:

1. I was tired of basketball.
2. I needed something to do after school.
3. It sounded like fun.
4. I wanted to be like Washerwoman.
5. My brother said Don't.
6. Liz Lampley (to spite her).
7. Eric Delong (to be near him).

Or was Mr. Cappelli right? Was I a freak? Some kind of oversexed teenage mutant female pervert?

I reached up to the bedstead and brought down Sidney, my snake. I wrapped it around my arm. Its green fur felt good. I let its red tongue tickle my nose. My father had won it for me at a fair when I was as little as P.K. Sidney had been taller than me.

That's what I wanted to do—go back, be little again. I remembered how I used to hide in my room with the door open just a crack, waiting to ambush my father. He would come down the hallway, and as soon as he took the first step on the stairs—"Charge!"—I would dart out and leap onto his back and ride him like my own personal horse—unless he happened to be an elephant or a camel that day—all the way down to the living room.

When I opened my eyes, the light was gone from under my door. The house was silent.

I had a sudden panicky thought. I got up and went downstairs, feeling my way. I flipped the switch for the light outside the front door. I didn't know how late it was, but what the heck, just in case Holly had a problem that was holding her up.

I went back to bed and listened for the doorbell.

In the morning I caught my father just as he took the first step down. He bellowed, I shrieked, and we both went swaying from wall to banister till he steadied out halfway down. He could have dumped me. He could have yelled, "You trying to kill me? You're too old for this." But he didn't. He just groaned, "Oh no," and let me ride him down.

In fact, for the first time ever, I rode him all the way into the kitchen.

Chapter Eleven

I'LL NEVER KNOW what I would have done if I hadn't seen George Bamberger after school on Monday. I was in the lobby, checking out the student art in the display case, when he came by.

"Where're you going?" I asked him.

"Home," he said.

"You have practice."

"I ain't going."

"Why?"

He looked at the kids going by. "I'm quitting."

I pulled him farther from the mob. "You can't quit."

He fiddled with his book bag. "Well, I am."

"Because he hollered at you Friday?"

"Nah. I just don't feel like it."

I shook him. It's so easy to bully seventh-graders. "George, you *can't* quit."

He stared at me. "Why not?"

I stared back. I couldn't think of an answer. So I asked a question of my own. "It's not because of me, is it?"

He chuckled. "Nah. You're no problem."

I loved him.

"George," I said, "you are not quitting."

He pulled away. "It's not up to you. It's up to me."

I re-grabbed him. "You're not quitting because I'm not quitting. I was going to. But now I'm not. I just found one person who says I'm not a problem, and I'm keeping you."

He whined. "I don't *want* to."

I put my arm around him. "Georgie, I need you. You need me." I steered him down the hallway. "You don't want to be a quitter, George. First you quit wrestling. Then what? School? Life?"

I expected the coach to say "Get out" when I stepped onto the scale, but all he said was, "One-oh-three."

Somebody did get out, though.

Kruko had just started leading us in exercises when a man showed up in the wrestling room. He stood in the corner with his arms folded, looking us over. His scowl was the best I had seen yet. Must have been a wrestler himself. When his eyes landed on me, he walked over to Coach Cappelli, and the two of them left.

Five minutes later Mr. Cappelli was back, calling "Zales! Here!"

Everybody was still. Bobby Zales walked off. But not straight off. He took a roundabout route that brought him past me. His shoulder slammed into mine. I would have toppled to the floor if George hadn't caught me. Zales said something too, but I couldn't make it out. Then he was gone.

"Monkey rolls!" yelled Kruko.

He headed straight for me. I knew the scowl on his face wasn't for wrestling, it was for me. Kruko and Zales were good buddies. I was set to monkey-roll with George and Burke, the other eighth-grade 105-pounder, but Kruko shoved the eighth-grader away. So now it was me, George, and Kruko.

Monkey rolls from hell!

Whenever Kruko was diving over me, he managed to drag his foot across me. When I was diving over him, his knee or elbow always seemed to be sticking in the air for me to smack into.

Mr. Cappelli hadn't come back yet, and the assistant, Mr. Paul, was gone that day.

The rolls went on and on. I prayed for the coach to return. I scrunched myself as small as I could on the rolls. When a Kruko foot raked my face, I couldn't take it anymore. In the middle of my next roll I shot up. I caught him in midair. He went cartwheeling and squawking onto his head.

In a split second we were on our feet, face-to-face, gasp to gasp, trying to catch our breaths in the sudden, high-ceiling silence of the room. His dark-brown unblinking eyes wanted to kill me. They were like two cameras that didn't just record but hated. A drop of sweat trickled down his forehead and over the ridge of his eyebrow till it snagged on his eyelash. I knew it could stay there forever and he would never blink it away.

The whistle blew. The coach was back.

"You're dead, Potter," Kruko muttered, and moved off.

I waited for Mr. Cappelli to tell me to take a hundred laps or a thousand push-ups or get out, but instead he grinned and said, "I can see you're all ready for action. Good. I like my wrestlers hungry. Good news today, people. What you've been waiting for – *live wrestling!*"

Cheers from the veterans.

George looked a little pale. "Don't worry," I whispered. "We'll wrestle each other."

We all grabbed headgear from a bin. You have to wear it when wrestling. There are two big plastic cups to cover your ears and a smaller one for your chin, all connected by adjustable straps – sort of like a bra for the ears. It took me a while to get mine on right.

First we learned what to do when you're the down person in the referee's position. Escapes, they're called. The coach taught us two of them, the sit-out and the stand-up. The idea for both is to be quick and to explode, especially on the stand-up. "Explode!" Coach Cappelli kept bellowing.

I exploded all right. I exploded an accidental elbow right into George Bamberger's face. His nose bled like a faucet. I jammed my sweatshirt sleeve in there. "Oh God, George, I'm sorry," I kept babbling. My one friend on the team, and I was trying to kill him.

By the time Mr. Cappelli showed up, I had George lying on the mat, his head back, my sweatshirt stuffed against his nose. Tears were streaming down his cheeks.

"What's this, General Hospital?" said the coach.

"I hit him with my elbow," I said. "His nose isn't broken, is it?"

"Did you pin him?"

"No. It was an accident."

The coach put his foot lightly on George's chest. "Slap the mat, Potter."

I gasped. "What?"

"*Slap the mat.*"

I slapped the mat.

"I said *slap* it, not pet it."

This time I really slapped it.

"There," he said. "Fall. You get a man down, you pin him. This isn't basketball, Potter." He lifted his foot. "Get up."

I helped George to his feet. The coach headed for the office. We followed. My one sleeve was soggy, so I switched arms. It was awkward, walking and keeping my sleeve under George's nose. Kids were snickering.

The coach turned. "Potter, outta here. Let him bleed for himself. You want to be a wrestler or a nurse?"

"Wrestler," I said.

"We'll find out," he sniffed, "soon as I get back."

He led George away.

Somebody yelled, "Showtime!"

The veterans started whistling and thumping the mats.

"All *right*!"

"Matburgers, baby, matburgers!"

"Let's *do* it!"

Somebody behind me called out, "Hey, who's she gonna beat up next?"

The whole place cracked up.

Chapter Twelve

MY LIVE WRESTLING OPPONENT was Burke, the other eighth grade 105-pounder. The ninth-grader had already gorged himself up to the 110-pound class. So with George Bamberger out, Burke was the only one my size left.

There isn't enough room for everybody to live-wrestle at once. There are always some sitters, some up. Burke and I were up.

"Okay," called the coach, "begin standing. *Wrestle!*" He blew his whistle.

I couldn't believe it. I was wrestling. Just like Washerwoman.

We shuffled, shuffled, circled, circled, butts down, heads up. Except for escapes, Mr. Cappelli hadn't actually taught us any moves yet. All he had said to everyone was, "Just go at it as best you can. That'll give me an idea of what I'm up against here." I scowled. Burke didn't even try. He looked terrified. He was a first-timer, like me, taller, but skinny.

"Let's go, people! This ain't the prom! Wrestle!" yelled the coach.

Burked gulped. He stuck out a hand and sort of pawed at me. I swiped it away. He stuck it out again. I palmed his face and shoved. He staggered backward into another pair of wrestlers, an amazed look on his face. I almost squealed with joy. I knew right then I was going to love wrestling. Washerwoman would have been proud.

Burke came back like somebody entering a tiger's cage. We circled some more. "C'mon," I whispered, "*do* something." But all he could do was circle, circle. From what I could see, nobody else was doing much more.

I wondered what Washerwoman would do. Would she jam her bucket over his head and bonk away with her own forehead? Would she go to the mop, dust his face for a while? Or maybe gross him out and pin him at the same time with her famous Sloppy Moppy? I wished I had a mop and a bucket.

"*Do* something, people!" roared the coach.

Okay, I thought, you asked for it.

I backed up a good ten feet. Burke stood stock still, making a perfect target, the moron. I charged. I leaped into the air, legs first. I turned sideways. I yelled, "Eeee-*yah!*" and I hit Burke smack-dab in the chest with the soles of both my feet. He staggered backward across the wrestling room, gaping, holding his chest like he'd just been shot. Guys moved out of the way. He didn't stop till he hit the wall.

Dead silence.

Everybody staring at me.

The coach came. Walking slowly. No big hurry. Eyes on the mat.

He stopped about five feet from me. Now his eyes were on me. He was working the whistle in his mouth like a cigar.

The whistle dropped. It bounced against his chest on its string. Then it was still.

"Potter," he said, "did you ever see a junior high school wrestling match?"

"No, sir," I said.

"Potter, have you ever seen a wrestling match of *any* kind?"

"Yes, sir."

"Where, Potter?"

"TV, sir."

The place cracked up, except for the coach. He blew the whistle.

"Saturday mornings? Main Event? That stuff, right?"

"Right."

"You got a favorite wrestler, Potter?"

"Uh, yes, sir."

"And who would that be, Potter?"

"Um . . . uh . . . Washerwoman?"

This time when everybody cracked up, the coach had to strain not to join them.

"Give her a mop!" somebody called.

The coach was chomping like a champ on his whistle. He took a deep breath. "Potter, this may come as a big surprise to you, but we don't wrestle like that here. That's Show Biz. We don't have body slams and head crunchers and kneecap stompers." He tilted his head. "Am I getting through to you?"

"Yes, sir."

"If you're gonna wrestle at Lenape Valley Junior High School, Potter, you're gonna wrestle the way the rest of us do. How's that sound?"

I nodded. "Okay."

He moved closer. "Sound good?"

"Yes, sir."

The coach pulled the whistle string over his head, turned away from me, and flipped it to someone. He turned back, he darted, and suddenly I was down, flat on my back. I could move my legs fine. My shoulders were the problem. They were clamped to the mat. I pushed. I couldn't move an inch.

I never felt so helpless in my life. I couldn't stand it. I panicked. I strained and pushed and twisted. I flailed my legs. I pressed down with my soles and made an arch of my body. I wiggled my fingers. Everything moved but my shoulders and upper arms. They were Krazy Glued to the mat.

As for the coach, I could hardly see him. Most of him was alongside of me. One of his arms was threaded through me somehow, so that my own arms crossed at the elbows. His hairy forearm was in my mouth. About the only thing I could see was the ceiling. It needed a new paint job.

The more I struggled, the more I got pasted into the mat. But I didn't stop trying. Maybe I tried too hard. I farted. It was just a quick little toot but it was enough to send the room into roars of laughter for the tenth time that day.

The coach was cool. He pretended he didn't notice. He let me up.

For a couple seconds, my arms wouldn't uncross.

"You okay, Potter?" he said.

"Yes, sir."

"People that make my team, Potter—which I wouldn't count on doing if I were you—*if* they're good enough, I teach them that hold. It's called a double arm tie-up. You never saw Washerwoman do that one, did you, Potter?"

"No, sir."

He pointed to the mat. "Down. Hands and knees. Referee's position."

I got down.

"Let's see if you learned anything. Delong—come here."

Oh my God.

"Okay, Delong, you're up. See if you can hold this wildcat."

I stared straight ahead into a blur of faces.

Eric Delong knelt with one knee beside me, his upper body leaning over me.

One hand curled around my elbow.

The other arm came around under me.

My muscles went into shock.

Mr. Cappelli stepped in front, inspecting. "Tighten it, Delong."

Eric Delong's arm got snugger around my waist. Fingertips were on my stomach. I could feel his chest on my back. I could feel his breath on the back of my neck.

Was the heartbeat I felt his or mine?

The whistle.

I froze.

Nothing happened.

Mr. Cappelli sagged.

"Potter, your job is to escape. Stand up. Sit out. *Explode.*"

I felt like saying: *But Coach, I don't want to escape.*

The whistle.

I exploded. I thought I was free, and I was, except for one wrist and one ankle. Whenever I tried to stand or get away, I flopped like a wounded duck.

The coach was in my face. "Escape, Potter! Escape!"

I went wild. I pushed, shoved, wrenched, kicked. I did everything but spit, and suddenly—I was out. Standing face-to-face with Eric Delong.

The whistle blew.

"Okay, first group, laps! Second group onto the mats! Let's go, people! Move!"

I went out with the first group. I ran the hallways in a daze.

Chapter Thirteen

I MADE THE TEAM!

I couldn't believe it. After wrestling Eric Delong on Monday, it had been downhill for the rest of the week.

The coach kept hollering at me and giving me extra laps.

The guys either laughed at me or ignored me.

George Bamberger came back to practice with a black eye, compliments of the nose bash I'd given him. He wrestled me because he had to, but that's all he did. He wouldn't talk to me. I didn't blame him. They were making fun of him in school: "Hey, there he is, the kid the *girl* beat up!"

I didn't do much better in the hallways myself. The first week there had been mostly stares. Now there were giggles and whispers and mouths twisted and ugly, like they had swallowed a worm.

Holly disappeared from my life.

As for Eric Delong, it was around Wednesday before the feel of his fingertips on my stomach went away. I didn't get to wrestle him again. I thought I saw him looking my way once or twice but he never came near and never said anything—except behind my closed eyes.

Before I went to sleep each night, or during homework, or sitting in class, or eating dinner—there he was, that cute, crinkly nose of his, that slightly smirky smile that seemed to say "Wouldn't you like to know what *I'm* thinking?" Sometimes we were bursting from the water at the pool. Sometimes—most of the times—we were in the referee's position on the mat, his arm curling around me, pressing tighter when Mr. Cappelli says, "Tighten it, Delong." And Mr. Cappelli never blew the whistle to start, and Eric Delong never took his arm away, and I never escaped.

Until I opened my eyes.

The only good thing they saw was that sheet of paper taped to the door of the wrestling room after practice on Friday. Everybody knew this was final cut day. Nobody took showers. At least, I didn't. It was change quick and join the mob at the door.

Down the left side of the sheet were the eighteen weight classes from 70 to 200 lb.

My name was after the 105. So was George Bamberger's.

Eric Delong's was after 130.

Out of the original fifty-five who went out for the team, forty made it. Eighteen would be varsity starters. The rest would be junior varsity backups.

I charged into the coach's office. He was leaning his chair way back, his feet on the desk. He was peeling an orange.

"Mr. Cappelli," I gasped, "is that list out there the kids that made it or didn't make it?"

He flipped an orange peel onto the desk. "That's my team. The Ravens."

"But *my* name's on it."

"That's right."

I still couldn't believe it. "You mean I made the team? There's no mistake?"

"Not that I know of."

I couldn't stand being still. I paced back and forth, saying "Man!" I stopped. I looked at him. "I thought I wasn't doing good. You said . . ."

"What I said last Friday?"

I nodded.

He pulled off the last peel. He broke the orange in half. I could smell it.

"Tell you a secret," he said. "You had the team made when you came in Monday, after me telling you to forget it."

"Really?"

He broke a wedge off. He offered it to me. I said No thanks. He popped it into his mouth. "One reason I said that stuff, to find out how bad you wanted it. And I wanted to give you a taste of the guff you're going to be hearing."

He held out another wedge. I shook it off. There was something I was wondering about all week. "What about Zales?" I said.

He sniffed. He shook his head. "Nothing for you to bother about. Man comes in here, tries to make a deal, tell me how to run my team." He shrugged. "It was the father's choice."

He ate a couple more wedges. The room reeked of orange. I sort of didn't want to leave. Like if I walked out—poof!—the spell would be broken, and my name would vanish from the list.

He gave me a half-grin. "Most of the time you're a pain in my butt, Potter. I wish you were a boy. If I had some better people, you would've been cut. As it is, you're the best 105-pounder I've got. So I'm stuck with you. Wrestling-wise, you don't know squat. I'm going to have to teach you everything I know just so you won't get pinned in the first ten seconds of every bout. And that's *if* we can find anybody to wrestle you."

He popped another wedge into his mouth. I wondered what he meant by that last statement.

He looked at me funny. He sighed. "But you don't have one thing I can't teach. You got moxie. Your mother was right about that. It's the only reason your name's on the list, Potter—you're a feisty little bugger."

He tossed his last orange wedge at me. I snatched it from the air. "Get outta here," he said.

I got out.

I floated out.

I crushed the orange wedge in my teeth. Sweetest juice there ever was.

Chapter Fourteen

$\mathbf{A}$T HOME there were four different reactions to the news.

P.K. jumped around the house screaming, "Maisie made it! Maisie made it!"

My mother didn't say a word. She just hugged me and gave my cheek such a long kiss, I thought I was getting my first hickey.

My father gave a small smile and said, "Congratulations," and shook my hand.

John made his little point with two words. "Congratulations, brother."

Nothing was going to ruin my mood. I gave him a big smile and patted him on the head. "Congratulations on making the basketball team, big bro. Great to be jocks, huh?"

I went to sleep happy that night. I dreamed of vans rolling through town with loudspeakers on their roofs announcing: *"Feisty little bugger makes wrestling team."*

I awoke next morning to strings swishing in my face and P.K. shouting, "Washerwoman! Washerwoman!"

Her beach bucket sat on her head like a yellow helmet and she was waving a toy mop. She jumped onto the bed. She straddled me. "Mop of *death*!" she snarled, and swabbed my face with the mop until I laid my shoulders flat to the mattress. "One—two—*three*!" she called. "You're pinned!" She rocked the bed, jumping. "Washerwoman wins! Washerwoman wins!"

I pulled her down onto the bed and put a Potter Special on her. It's my own invention. You just tickle your opponent till they give up, which she finally did after laughing herself purple.

Then we turned on the TV and watched the real Washerwoman go to war with Ma Barker and The Floozie.

After lunch I headed down to St. Jude's. Specifically to the parish school gym that they open up to kids on Saturday afternoons. This was my first time since the last winter. I used to be a regular.

Snow flurries were blowing by the time I got there. I could hear basketballs inside. Tina McIntire was coming out as I was going in. We high-fived (actually, it was a low-five for her, being so tall). "Kick some butt, Maypot," she said.

The St. Jude's gym doubles as an auditorium. There are two baskets. The one in front of the stage had a game going. At the other one, kids were just shooting around. I had my ball with me. I bounced it a couple times and headed over.

It was mostly Lenape Valley kids—three girls from the junior high basketball team and some guys. One of the girls was Holly Gish. One of the guys was Eric Delong.

Everybody acted cool. They kept on shooting, like they didn't know I was there. I stopped outside the key, about twenty feet from the basket. I let it fly. *Swish*, nothing but net. I hadn't touched a basketball in almost a year. Pure luck.

I joined the others under the basket, shagging rebounds. Holly brushed by, sneering, "Thought you didn't like basketball."

I was glad she didn't wait for an answer. I wasn't sure myself why I was there. Could it possibly be because I remembered that Eric Delong hung out there some Saturdays?

After a while somebody said, "Let's shoot for sides."

We did. There were eleven of us. The first ten to make their foul shots played. The eleventh sat. That was Toni Briscoe. She would get in the next game.

Holly was on the other team. I guarded her. I resisted the temptation to guard Eric, who was also on the other team. He wore a cut-off Penn State T-shirt and sweatpants.

Holly kept lowering her shoulder and driving on me. I could have called foul every time but I didn't. Usually by the time she reached the basket the ball was gone, because I had flicked it away. Holly never was very quick.

The shots I got I mostly created for myself, since no one passed me the ball. I didn't let it bother me. Nothing was going to spoil my good mood over making the wrestling team. It was a crime, the number I did on Holly. I drove around her, shot over her, did everything but bounce in two points off her head.

At the end of the game, we looked for Toni Briscoe. She was gone. So we played on. We kept playing games of ten baskets until players started drifting home.

When it got down to four, we decided to play H-O-R-S-E. There was me, Eric, Holly, and a kid named Matt Williams.

Holly followed me. I started her off with my patented jump shot. She missed. H for her.

Four more shots—O-R-S-E—and Holly was history. Matt Williams, not a very good shot, kept missing too.

A couple of minutes later it was down to me and Eric, each with only an H.

I was heading for my favorite spot for the next shot when I noticed we had a visitor. Liz Lampley. I wondered how long she had been there. She was standing just inside the door. She had on a quilted jacket and boots. The boots had snow on them. Holly and Toni Briscoe were standing next to her. They weren't talking, just watching.

I guess I got a little rattled, because I missed my shot. Eric made his. I missed, so I was losing with H-O.

That was the last shot I missed. I wasn't about to get beaten at basketball by a football player and a wrestler. He missed his next one.

I bumped him to H-O with a fifteen-foot jumper.

R was a tap-in off the backboard.

S was a bomb from dead in the corner.

I finished him off with a driving hook. Left-handed.

"Another game?" I said.

He wasn't listening.

He was whipping the ball against the nearest wall. If the ball had been a watermelon, it would have splattered for miles. As it was, it *poinged* off and went rolling down to the stage end of the court. I ran it down. When I looked back, they were all gone.

I put on my jacket and left. Outside, the snow was up to my sneaker tops. By the time I got home, my feet were wet and cold.

The phone was ringing.

It was Holly. My first thought was, *Great, she's back!*

She wasn't.

She said, "Maisie, I thought you were acting like a jerk before. Now you're a *stupid* jerk."

"You called to tell me that?"

She laughed. "And you don't even *know* you're being stupid."

"Fill me in."

"First of all, you don't know *anything* about guys."

"That so?"

"You don't go beating them in sports if you want them to like you. If you think Eric is ever going to like you after what you did today, you're crazy."

"Maybe you're jealous because *you're* not good enough to beat a guy."

"Maybe *you* should've seen how Eric was hanging all over Liz on the way home today."

"Maybe *you're* sucking up to Liz yourself."

"Maybe *you* blew it, girl."

"Maybe *you're* just mad because I blew *you* away on the court today." I called into the phone: "Hey, Lizard! You there?"

The phone went *click*. Twice.

I went upstairs. I pulled off my sneaks and socks. My mother came in, noticed that my toes were pink from cold, and held them in her hands. "Feel better?"

I nodded.

"You don't look too happy."

I shrugged.

"I thought you'd still be in a good mood over making the team."

"Guess it wore off."

She rubbed my feet and looked at me for a while. She nodded. "I think it's time we got you that pet."

I stared at her. "What pet?"

"The one you said you wanted."

"Mom, that was years ago. In third grade."

"Well, I'm just getting around to answering requests from that year."

"You did answer me then. You said no. You said I wouldn't take care of it and it would poop all over."

"Ask me again."

"No."

"No, you won't ask me, or no, you don't want a pet?"

"No everything."

She nodded. "I'll take that as a yes. We'll go to the pet shop at the mall tomorrow." She patted my feet and left the room.

Chapter
Fifteen

MY MOTHER dropped me at Pawn 'N Jaws while she went off shopping.

The dogs were cute. I wanted them all. I did not want to have to take care of one.

The kittens were cute. But every kitten I've known grew up to be a snooty cat.

I wandered to the back, where the little dudes hung out, like hamsters and gerbils. There were mice too, about twenty of them in a glass tank. They were funny to watch, hyper, scampering, jumping, climbing up the water bottle. They were great wrestlers, so quick it was hard to follow them.

The next tank had only one in it. At first I thought it was a big mouse, but the sign said YOUNG RATS.

It was two colors, gray and white. Gray down to the shoulders then white the rest of the way except for a gray stripe down the back. I had seen cats like that. The word *pretty* occurred to me, then I thought, Nah, can't be, it's a *rat*. And anyway, what was a rat doing in a pet shop?

I was ready to move on to the guinea pigs when the rat stopped me. It got up from the back corner of the tank, walked over to me, stood up with its little pink hands against the glass, and looked at me. I mean, the hamsters and gerbils, when I got close to their tanks, they all ran to the back and huddled in a quivering bunch. Now here comes this rat doing everything but talk to me.

"Is that all you got?" a voice behind me said.

"That's the last one," said another voice.

I moved aside. The first voice belonged to some weird kind of cowboy. He wore boots, jeans, a black T-shirt, a wide-brim hat with a feather, a ring on his thumb, and tattoos all over his arms. The other voice was a salesgirl.

"Ain't nothin' but a runt," said the cowboy.

"It's still young," said the salesgirl. "About six weeks old."

"Hardly make an appetizer. Any more comin' in?"

"With rats, we never know. We don't get a steady supply."

"Rambo's a growin' boy. He needs a rat a week."

The rat was still standing against the glass, looking at the two of them, friendly as could be.

I turned to the cowboy. "Who's Rambo?"

His feathered hat never moved. His eyeball slid to the corner of his eye. I thought he wasn't going to answer but then he started to grin. He pulled out his wallet. He pulled out a picture. He handed it to me.

"There's Rambo."

Rambo was a snake.

I locked eyes with the salesgirl.

"I'll take the rat," I said.

She smiled.

"Hey—" said the cowboy.

I gave him back his picture. "Tell Rambo to go eat a meatball."

It cost me $1.99.

I waited outside the shop for my mother.

"You're through looking?" she said.

"Yep."

She saw the bag. "Watcha got?"

"My pet."

"You bought one?"

"Only cost a dollar ninety-nine."

She looked at the bag some more. "It's not a fish."

"Nope."

I opened the bag. She peeked in. She squawked and jumped back.

"Don't worry," I told her. "She's friendly. The girl said it's a her. She's a hooded rat, because of the gray upper part."

She stayed five feet away. "You *bought* it? *Here?*"

"Some guy was gonna feed her to his snake. She's still young. She's like, in rat years, a teenager."

She just stared.

On the way home, I had to sit in the backseat with the rat. I'm sure if I offered to ride in the trunk, my mother would have accepted gladly.

I called the rat Bernadette. I called her that because Bernadette is my favorite name and I got tired of waiting for a human friend to come along who had it.

I kept her in an old ten-gallon glass tank that once held John's goldfish. But I let her out a lot, like on my bed and bookcase and mainly on my desk during homework.

She would climb in and out of my shirt, up my arm, sit on my head. She made a den out of an empty Kleenex box. She furnished it with tissues, rubber bands, pencils, erasers, pizza crusts—anything she could lug into the box. She loved to climb into the top desk drawer and ride it as I pulled it in and out. One time she peed in my paper-clip tray, but otherwise she was pretty good.

I loved to watch her sleep. With her head bowed in to meet her feet and her tail curled around, she slept in a perfect circle.

Except for P.K. ("I want one too!"), nobody in the family liked Bernadette. Neither did most people who came to the house.

"*Eewwww!*" they would go. "A RAT!"

The same tone of voice I'd hear about a girl going out for wrestling.

Chapter Sixteen

THINGS WENT PRETTY SMOOTH the first couple of days at practice. A lot of drills, a lot of running.

Each day Mr. Cappelli taught the rookies a new move. First we did takedowns. Then we learned wrist and ankle control.

And then one day he said the magic word.

"Okay, Ravens, today we do a basic control move. The crotch ride."

Was it my imagination, or did everybody stop breathing just then?

The coach called Kruko up to help him demonstrate. So here was the scene: Mr. Cappelli putting the move on Kruko . . . Mr. Cappelli saying, Now you do *this* . . . Now you do *this* . . . and the whole place getting tenser and tenser. Meanwhile, I'm trying to picture myself doing it. I guess the closest I ever came was when I had to change P.K.'s diaper.

As the coach explained to us rookies, you don't go around pinning anybody with just a crotch ride. It's a control step on the way to a pinning hold, such as a half-nelson. "The point is," he said, "you can't go very far in wrestling without sooner or later jamming your arm between somebody's legs."

The demonstration ended. Time for the rest of us to try it.

Up till then I had usually been partnered with George Bamberger. Not that we didn't have a choice. Mr. Cappelli encouraged us to practice out of our weight classes, especially with heavier people. But every time he blew his whistle to start, everybody but George fanned out from me like I had terminal B.O.

This time Mr. Cappelli made it an order: every other weight class had to move up one, which for me and George meant up to 110 pounds. That's how come I was facing Beans Agway.

And that's all I did, face him. Because while everybody else was riding a crotch or getting theirs ridden, all me and Beans did was gawk at each other. He folded his arms. I folded my arms. I sure wasn't going to make the first move.

When Mr. Cappelli showed up, he growled. "You two playing games with me?"

"I want to wrestle," I told him. "He won't."

Beans snarled, "I ain't wrestlin' no chick,"

I thought for a second Mr. Cappelli was going to pinch Beans's head off. But he didn't move, he didn't say anything. He just glared for a while. Then he blew his whistle. Not that he needed to. Everybody had already stopped.

The coach just stood there for a minute, slumpy, looking down at the blue mat, letting air out between his teeth. Suddenly he grabbed me by the arm and hauled me up front with him. He growled, "Stand here," and flung my arm back to me. I was thinking, *Hey what did I do?* But I figured I better shut up.

The coach whispered something to Mr. Paul, who left the room. Then he started talking.

"I didn't want to do this. I was hoping my team would be mature enough to deal with it without me having to make a speech. But"— he shrugged—"you want a speech, you got a speech."

"The speech has three parts. Part number one." He grabbed my wrist. He held up my arm. "This"—he waggled my arm—"this is *not* a girl. This is *not* a female. This is a *wrestler*. Period. There are no boys on my team. There are no girls on my team. There are wrestlers. That's all." He shook my arm again. "Wrestler. Got it?" He cupped his hand to his ear. "I *said*, Got it?"

The team roared back: "Got it!"

He let go of me.

"Part number two. *I* decide who faces who around here. Anybody refuses to face this wrestler, you're off the team. Gone. Got it?"

"Got it!"

He gave me a light push that sent me back to the mat.

"Part number three. This is called a desensitizing exercise, Ravens. As far as I'm concerned—as far as *you're* concerned—there is no difference between a crotch and an elbow, except where they're located. Crotches, elbows, wrists, ankles—they all have one meaning on the mat. They're control points. That's all. Right?"

"Right!"

"All right. Repeat after me. Crotch."

"Crotch!"

"Louder."

"*Crotch!*"

"Agway, let me hear you."

"Uh, crotch."

"Yell it, Agway!"

"Crotch!"

"Bamberger."

"Crotch!"

"Kruko."

"Crotch!"

"Potter."

"Crotch!"

He called every kid on the team.

Then he was like a teacher talking to first-graders. "Okay group, everybody that does not have a crotch, raise your hand."

His eyebrows went up.

"Well, well. Let's try it this way. Everybody who does have a crotch, hands up."

All hands went up.

"Anybody have more than one?"

Laughs. A couple hands shot up.

The coach grinned. "So, everybody's got at least one, right? Seems these crotch things are pretty damn common, right? . . . *Right?*"

"Right!"

Somebody blurted out: "Dolly!"

Mr. Paul was returning with Dolly slung over his shoulder.

Dolly is the life-size dummy for learning CPR on. You don't get to meet Dolly till ninth grade Health, but everybody in school knows who she is. It's a mystery how the dummy came to be called Dolly, since it doesn't really look like one sex or another.

Mr. Cappelli dragged Dolly onto the mat and dumped her in front of Beans. "Okay, Agway, you don't want to wrestle a chick? How about a dummy? Crotch-ride."

Beans just gawked at the coach.

"Let's go, Agway. It's a piece of plastic. You afraid of plastic too?"

Real slow, Beans sank to his knees. He stayed that way for a while, staring at Dolly.

"Crotch-ride, Agway. You want to show me where the crotch is?"

Agway pointed.

"Okay, now grab it. Crotch-ride."

Agway grabbed it. He crotch-rode, pretty sloppily.

Mr. Cappelli made him stay with it till he got it right. Beans jumped up the instant it was over. Mr. Cappelli applauded. Everybody else joined in, cheering and whistling. Beans grinned and took a bow.

Mr. Cappelli called out five or six others to crotch-ride the dummy. More cheers and whistles. Pretty soon it sounded more like a party than a practice.

I prayed the coach wouldn't ask me to do it. He did. I took a deep gulp and crotch-rode the dummy. I made sure I did it right the first time. Cheers and whistles for me.

Mr. Cappelli picked up the dummy and tossed it back to Mr. Paul. He was in a good mood now. "All right, Ravens, one more time. Crotch."

"Crotch!"

"Can't hear you, Ravens."

"*Crotch!*"

"Make me proud!"

"C R O T C H!"

Chapter Seventeen

THINGS CHANGED.

Suddenly George Bamberger didn't want to wrestle me. Every time I looked for him, he was paired off with someone else. I wondered if he was mad because I was the varsity starter and he was JV backup.

It didn't matter too much, though. Because of an even bigger change: everybody else did want to wrestle me.

Not only that, I was going great against them, better than I had ever expected. I thought guys would be pinning me all over the place, if only because most of them were stronger and more experienced. But I seemed to have more natural ability than I realized. I was quick and slippery. They even gave me a nickname: Slime. I kept getting out of their holds. I started shooting moves of my own. I hadn't known I was that strong.

In fact, I almost got a couple of pins.

When you're wrestling in practice, sometimes one of the sitters will play referee. He scrunches his face to the mat and looks for shoulder blades. If both of them are touching for just one second—not three like on TV—he hits the mat with the palm of his hand. *Thump!* It's a pin. Or as they also call it, a fall. Or as they also call it, showing the other guy the lights.

Well, a couple of times I had guys down on one shoulder blade, but they got away. I made a vow that before the season started, I was going to pin somebody in practice.

Off the mat, though, things weren't going so good.

I kept remembering what Holly said about blowing my chances with Eric Delong by beating him in H-O-R-S-E. I thought about how I smoked him in the hallway race the first day of practice. And how I escaped from him the time Mr. Cappelli put us together on the mat.

Was Holly right?

Was I stupid?

I took Bernadette out of her glass apartment. I took her little front feet between my fingers and stood her up. I brought my face close to hers. "Can a boy like a girl he loses to?" I asked her. She leaned out and with her tiny pink tongue she licked my nose like a puppy.

One day on the way to practice, I passed Jeff Beman and Amy Wisenthal making out in a stairwell. Two years before, I wasn't the best girl athlete in sixth grade. Amy was. In fact, at Field Day, she won more events than anybody, boy or girl. The only reason I won Outstanding Seventh Grade Female Athlete the following year was because Amy didn't go out for anything but field hockey.

The next year—*fsssst.* Amy traded in her hockey stick for lipstick. The only fast break she ever runs anymore is into Jeff Beman's clutches. Amy Wisenthal. She could have gone to college on a scholarship. Maybe made the pros. Olympics. All she became was a world-class smoocher. If there was a law against kissing, she'd be on death row.

Was that how it had to be? One or the other?

I wished I could talk to Holly about all this. I was getting constipation of the brain, keeping it inside. I hated her. I missed her. I missed our Friday overnights. I missed being that close to someone.

And then, for one night at least, I was.

I was hanging around the refrigerator Friday night when my mother said, "Haven't seen Holly in a while. She coming over tonight?"

I stabbed a pickle in the Vlasic jar. "No."

"You going there?"

I pulled the pickle out. "No."

She didn't say anything. Maybe if she had, I wouldn't have started to cry.

"Close the jar," she said. "Pickle juice and tears don't mix."

I closed the jar. She sat at the table. "You meant it that night, Holly hates you."

I nodded.

"Want to tell me?"

I bit the pickle. Juice ran down my chin. My nose was dripping. My eyes were watering. For all I knew, my ears were leaking.

"Goodness *gwayshus!*" She got up, tore off a paper towel, and swabbed me till I was mostly dry. She sat back down. "So?"

"So Holly dumped me."

"So why?"

"Oh, you know."

"Wrestling, you mean?"

"She traded me in for Liz Lampley."

"Liz Lampley . . . You mentioned her before?"

"She's a cheerleader. Gorgeous face. Gorgeous body. Other than that, she's ugly."

"So what does Liz Lampley have to do with anything?"

I took another bite. "It's a long story."

She took the Vlasic jar and my fork and stabbed a pickle for herself. "I have all night."

"Mom," I said, "this isn't mother-daughter stuff. This is best-friend stuff."

"Best-friend-your-own-age-up-in-your-room-with-the-door-shut stuff?"

"Exactly."

We sat there staring and chewing at each other for a while. Then I got up and went to my room.

A half hour later there was a knock on my door. Usually I just say "Come in," but I didn't feel like company, so I said, "Who is it?"

"Ellen," came the answer in my mother's voice.

Ellen is her first name. It was weird, hearing her call herself that. I wondered what the joke was.

"Come in," I said.

The door opened. There stood my mother, a big grin on her face, a scarf around her neck, and an overnight bag hanging from her shoulder. She gave me a window-washer wave. "Hi! I'm Ellen Lupinski, your *best friend*. I am thir*teen*, and I have come to stay over*night* with *you*!"

"Close the door," I told her. "You're embarrassing me." She closed it. "I'm not in the mood for all this."

She dumped the bag on my bed. "You're in the mood for an overnight with your best friend, Ellen Lupinski, aren't you?"

"Mom —"

"Ellen."

"*Mom*. *Back to the Future* was a movie. This is real. Besides, when you were thirteen, you were probably a nerd."

"No," she said, "actually, I was cool. I only became a nerd later."

She flung her scarf to the floor.

"Mom, scram."

"Ellen."

"Mo-om!"

She opened the overnight bag. She took out a Sea World night-shirt and a pack of cards. Holly and I always played Hearts for part of the night. She kicked off her shoes. She climbed onto the bed. She bounced up and down on her knees. She threw my pillow at my face.

"I'm warning you," I told her, "there's a rat in this room." I knew she was still shaky about my roommate.

She gave Bernadette a nervous glance and turned back to me. "I said I was your best friend. Would I allow a wild beast to come between us? Now say it. Ellen."

"No."

"Ellen."

"No."

To get her off my back, I finally said it. From then on, whenever I said "Mom," she would look at the ceiling until I changed it to "Ellen."

Pretty soon we were playing Hearts and making microwave pizza and doing all the things I usually did with Holly. She giggled and laughed and made faces and said prehistoric stuff like "Holy catfish!" and "Far out!"

She told me about the times she got dumped—by girlfriends, by boyfriends, and even, once, by a hamster, who liked her brother Harry better. A couple times, she said, she did the dumping, and that wasn't any easier. "It's just as hard to be the dumper as the dumpee," she said.

We laughed at that and brought up the pickle jar, and before long I was spilling my guts about Eric Delong. The whole mess, starting from the day at the pool.

I told her what Holly had said, how I blew it by beating him in H-O-R-S-E.

"*Was* I stupid?" I asked her.

She said she didn't think so. She said winning and losing really shouldn't have anything to do with it, and if a boy can't handle getting beat by a girl, well, that's his problem. And he probably wasn't worth it anyway.

"Is he why you went out for wrestling?" she said.

"Everybody at school thinks so."

"What do you think?"

I sighed. "I'm trying not to think."

By the time we ran out of gas, it was almost two in the morning. We put our nightshirts on, turned out the light, and crawled under the covers.

"Aren't you afraid your boyfriend down the hall will get jealous?" I said.

"That dork? I'm dumping him."

We laughed. Then we were quiet.

We lay in the darkness, which smelled of pickles and pizza. After a while, she gave a sleepy little girl kind of yawn and turned over on her side.

"'Night, Maisie."

"'Night, Ellen . . . Say good-night to Bernadette."

Silence. Then: " 'Night, Bernadette."

Chapter Eighteen

So NATURALLY, brilliant person that I am, I took all that good advice and dumped it down the crapper.

The next day, Saturday, I went back to St. Jude's for some basketball. It was pretty much the same scene as before, with one colossal exception: Luscious Liz was there from the start. And this time she wasn't on the sidelines.

Thanks to her, we almost never got to the game. After sides were picked, Lizard started pulling off her jeans. Somebody whistled, and another somebody called, "Take it off!" And the next thing you knew, she was up on the stage.

The audience became a gang of chimpanzees, not just the guys but the girls too, hooting and whistling and clapping. It seemed that it took an hour for each leg to slither out of the jeans. The place went wild when she held them over her head, showing off her pink-and-aqua short shorts. The joint exploded when she puckered her red lips and flung the jeans down to them. Then more of the same while she stripped her sweatshirt off. I kept hoping the priest would drop by, but no such luck.

Finally the game began.

Imagine a rock trying to play basketball. Now imagine a clumsy rock. That's how useful Lady Longlegs was on the court. She refused to dribble the ball because she might break a fingernail. So she would just lug it to her favorite spot, one inch from the basket. Then she would squat down, lunge up, and heave the ball underhanded with a cutesy, peepy little grunt. The ball would either go straight up in the air or over the backboard.

To me, it was sickening. Everybody else thought she was adorable.

The real action happened whenever Eric made a shot. Then Lizard Liz would go squealing and jiggling and jumping all over him.

Like before, Holly and I guarded each other. It was a war, more like football than basketball. I was surprised she could be so physical. I got the impression she had appointed herself bodyguard for the Lovely One. Once, when Her Supreme Lipness was squatting to do her cutesy underhand peep shot, I switched off and swatted the ball up onto the stage. Luscious gave a horrified squawk and glanced around for Eric. Holly gave me a sneak jab in the back. I bit my tongue. I figured if I punched her, they'd all attack me at once.

It was getting harder and harder to tell Holly and Lizard apart. Holly was now wearing the same ton of makeup as Lizard and had her hair the same way. They both wore these hoop earrings that were so huge I kept wanting to shoot the ball through them.

Once again the afternoon came down to a game of H-O-R-S-E. Except this time, Eric wanted to make it longer. So I suggested we play H-I-P-P-O-P-O-T-A-M-U-S. Me, Holly, Lizard, Eric, and a St. Jude's kid.

There are twelve letters in hippopotamus. Legs was gone in twelve shots.

Then Holly went.

Then the St. Jude's kid.

Again, me and Eric Delong. The last two.

I had gotten off to a blazing start, and by this time, Eric already had H-I-P-P-O-P-O-T. I only had H-I-P. I was licking my chops for the kill when a tiny voice hissed in my ear: *Stupid. Look what you're doing. You're not winning. You're losing—him.*

So I started missing.

I kept missing until I lost.

And when I got the final S—surprise!—my world didn't change one bit.

What did I expect? Eric hugging me and sweeping me off my feet and shouting: "Oh thank you, Maisie! Thank you for letting me win! Now I'm free to love you!"

Right.

What I got was him shouting, "Yeah!" and whipping the ball to the ceiling. He strutted out the door with Lizard and Holly mobbing him like he had just slain the dragon.

I have felt rotten plenty of times in my life. But this was a different kind of rotten. It came from me. Like I had barfed all over myself. And what was worse, I couldn't wipe it off.

At practice Monday, for the first time ever, I didn't try very hard.

I just went through the motions, waiting for someone to throw me out with the garbage. I couldn't even bring myself to look at Eric Delong.

I guess we were about halfway through the live wresting when I started having a funny feeling, a feeling that something was going on but I didn't know what. At the time I was wrestling a ninth-grader, Jerry McCann. Even though he was three weight classes above me and I was hardly trying, I kept getting near falls on him. And he didn't look too broken up about it.

I thought about how well I had been doing against these guys in practice since I made the team. About how surprisingly good I was. Or was I?

Next I went against Beans Agway—and pinned him in ten seconds with a chicken wing and arm bar. I forgot my mood and jumped up like a winning gladiator. My first-ever pin! Showed him the lights! "Yeah!" I shouted.

And then others were joining in, pumping their fists, cheering. But cheering *me?*

Because now that funny little feeling was like a bear roaring in my ear.

I looked around. The coaches were out of the room. Everybody, wrestlers and sitters, was cheering, but it wasn't me they were looking at.

It was Beans.

They were cheering him.

And it wasn't only cheering. Laughing was there too. I looked down and saw Beans laughing hardest of all, his shoulders still pinned to the mat—and suddenly it all came clear.

Two days earlier, at St. Jude's, I had been Beans—a loser *on purpose*.

All of a sudden Beans stopped laughing—right after I punched him in the mouth. And then we were rolling on the mat, and then the coaches were pulling us apart. Mr. Cappelli was yelling at me but I didn't hear because I was yelling right back, nose to nose. He stopped first, and that's when I heard myself scream: "I want the Nutcracker!"

Chapter Nineteen

THE COACH LOOKED AT ME LIKE, Where did you escape from?

"Forget it," he said.

"No," I told him, "you forget it. Your way doesn't work. I'm just a joke to them. They don't even try against me. I don't care if they don't like me. I just want to be treated like a member of the team. Maybe I don't scowl enough. Maybe I don't wear a jockstrap. But I'm a Raven too! I'm not a joke!"

I shoved Agway. He shoved me back, right into Mr. Cappelli. I bounced off and told him pointblank: "Nutcracker, or I quit."

He stared at me. I could have changed my clothes and been halfway home by the time he said, his lips barely moving, "Okay."

Agway piped, "I'm first!"

"I'm second!" called Kruko.

The way the Nutcracker works, the Nut—that was me—gets to wrestle ten people in a row. You wrestle each one of them for thirty seconds or until somebody gets pinned. So the longest you could wrestle would be ten times thirty seconds, or three hundred seconds—five minutes. In wrestling, that's an eternity. Junior high bouts last only four minutes at the most.

In a normal year, only one or two guys are nuts enough to be Nuts. Usually they're ninth-graders.

The Nut doesn't pick the opponents. They volunteer and they can be any weight.

After Agway and Kruko volunteered, Mr. Cappelli said, "Line up."

Half the team stampeded into line. You would have thought Liz Lampley was giving away free kisses.

I was boiling inside. I was almost jumping out of my headgear. I wanted to rumble. I just stared at Agway. His shoulders were twitching. His cheekbone was red from my punch. He wanted to kill me.

Good, I thought.

There was a scuffle behind him in the line. Probably guys fighting for the tenth spot.

The whistle blew.

We charged into each other. No dancing around. No shuffle, shuffle, circle, circle. We thundered to the mat. I forgot what little I knew about wresting. I was just fighting.

He was strong. This wasn't the same Beans Agway I had pinned a couple of minutes before. I could see now how much he had been faking, how much all of them had, and it just made me madder. I reached for a leg. I grabbed it, and suddenly I was on my back.

Thump! went the coach's hand.

"Next."

I knew from the coach calling out the time that Agway had pinned me in ten seconds. As he walked off, Kruko whispered to him, "Stupid."

I wondered what that was about.

The whistle blew.

Kruko flew into me, and next thing I knew I was on his shoulders like a sack of potatoes. It was the fireman's carry, a takedown hold I had seen but hadn't learned yet. I knew what was coming—oof!—I was dumped to the mat, all 145 of Kruko's pounds landing on me. But he didn't go for the pin. He rolled off and jumped up and motioned with his hands, "Come on . . . come on." And now I knew what he had meant by "Stupid." Agway had finished me off too fast. Kruko wanted to stretch it out.

Mr. Cappelli was calling down the seconds: ". . . twenty . . . fifteen . . . ten . . ."

If I was smart, I would have shuffled and danced away from Kruko. But I kept tearing into him and getting myself hoisted and whammed to the mat. The third time down he stayed on me for the pin—*thump!* —just as Mr. Cappelli called. "Thirty! Next!"

It's kind of blurry in my memory from then on. I remember one kid putting an arm crush on me, yanking down on my wrist while driving his head up under my armpit. After that I was pretty much down to one arm. My headgear kept twisting, so I'd have this ear flap covering my face.

Each time Mr. Cappelli said "Next," I hoped to see the 70-pounder stepping up but they were all big. In fact, one of them was the heavyweight, Henry Epps, who tipped the scales at a cool 200. A whale. He didn't even bother to put a move on me. He just flung me down, flopped on top of me, and that was that.

"Next . . ."

"Next . . ."

"Next . . ."

Ceiling lights . . . ceiling lights . . .

And then Mr. Cappelli was in front of me, saying, "That's it."

I remember putting my hands on his chest and pushing, but he didn't move. "No," I told him. "I'm not done." He had this funny look on his face. He reached for me. I pushed away. I turned, I reached for the gang of faces watching, wavering, tilting . . .

Chapter Twenty

FIRE IN THE BRAIN!

I opened my eyes.

There was the old familiar peeling-paint ceiling. The lights.

Was I being pinned again?

Then Mr. Cappelli's face covering the lights. Mr. Cappelli smiling. "You awake, Tiger?"

His hand under my nose . . .

Fire in the brain!

I jerked away. Sat up. He handed a broken blue capsule to someone. Smelling salts.

I tried to stand. He held me down. "Sit for a minute." His voice was soft.

There was a bloody towel in his hand.

"I hurt somebody?" I asked him.

He chuckled. "You might say that."

When he finally let me up, he kept hold of my arm. "I'm okay," I told him. The mat felt like a water bed.

There was clapping. I wondered why.

"Way to go, Nut," somebody said.

I felt pats on my back. George Bamberger was alongside of me, smiling. He touched my shoulder. "Good going."

Somebody grabbed my hand and shook it. I turned. I couldn't believe it. "Beans?"

"You okay, Raven?" he said.

"Yeah."

"Good."

He tapped me on the butt, like I was a guy.

Then I was sitting in the coach's office, in his chair, listening.

"I don't know whether to be mad at you or at myself for letting you get away with that, Potter. I guess I'll be satisfied as long as you can walk out of here tonight. This is all as new to me as it is to you. I'm making it up as we go along. I let you do that because I thought something drastic was called for and I didn't have any better ideas."

He took a long breath. He shook his head. "Okay. Come here." I came there. He held three fingers in front of my face. "How many?"

"Three."

"What day is it?"

"Monday."

"What's your middle name?"

"I'm not telling. I hate it."

"Who's your favorite wrestling coach?"

"Anybody but you."

I brushed him aside and walked out of the office. He was laughing.

The moment I walked into the locker room, everything came to a standstill. The half-naked girls' basketball team was gawking at me.

Tina McIntire stepped out of the shower and stopped dead. "What happened to *you?*"

I crawled to the nearest mirror. I looked like a victim from *Friday the 13th*. There was blood on my sweatshirt and more caked on my right ear. There was a mat burn on one cheek. The rest of my face was waxy and splotchy.

But the winner was my upper lip. It looked like somebody had planted a golf ball inside it. I looked like a fish. I opened my mouth. I looked more like a fish.

I dragged my carcass to my locker. I slumped to the bench. After a while I got bored with staring at the floor, so I figured I'd tackle a sneaker. I pulled the bow on one lace loose, but that's as far as I got. Long, thin, brown hands came into view. Tina finished untying the lace. Then she untied the other one. She pulled my sneaks off, and my socks.

She kept muttering, "I hope you're not doing this for him . . . I hope you're not, girl."

She got the rest of my clothes off. She steered me to the showers. She turned on a shower and nudged me under it. She stuck a bar of soap in my hand. "That's as far as I go," she said.

Once I was under the water, I didn't want to leave. Tina dragged me out, gave me towel. The rest of the team was gone.

She hoisted my arms and rolled her deodorant on me. She got me dressed and walked out with me. Until recently, Tina McIntire and I had been mostly sports acquaintances, teammates. It was starting to feel like something more.

Mr. Cappelli was in the hallway.

"No practice for you tomorrow," he said. "Don't let me see your face till Wednesday." George Bamberger was with him. "This is your escort home tonight."

Tina said, "I'll take care of her."

"I want a wrestler along," said the coach. "Make sure you don't abduct her over to the basketball team."

"That's funny," I mumbled past the golf ball in my mouth. "A couple weeks ago *you* told me to go out for basketball."

He stomped his foot and scared us halfway down the hall. "Out!"

So that's how I came to be escorted home by Tina on one side of me and George on the other.

"Who are *you?*" Tina said when we got outside.

"George Bamberger," he said.

She screeched, "*Hamburger?*"

"Bam," he said, all serious.

Poor George, I thought. Tina could eat him alive. But she wouldn't.

She would toy with him, though.

"What weight?" she asked him.

"One-oh-five."

"Same as fat lip here?"

"Yeah."

"She's varsity, you're JV, right?"

"Yeah."

"So she's better than you."

George shrugged. "Guess so."

We came to a street. Tina took my arm like I was an old lady. "Think you can make it across, ma'am?"

I shoved her away. She laughed.

"So, Hamburger," she said, "how's that make you feel? Can't beat a girl out."

Silence from George.

"He handles it," I said.

I looked at him. "Now I know why you wouldn't wrestle me lately. You didn't want to join in the little joke." He shrugged. "You could have told me, though. What they were doing."

He looked away. He nodded. "I know."

Tina bent into my face. "You done? Now you be quiet while we're talkin' about you." She straightened up. "So . . . Hamburger . . . what do you think? She's going to do it?"

George looked up at her. "Do what?"

"Catch her lover boy. Delong."

George turned away. He didn't answer.

"Must have the hots for that boy something awful, you think, Ham? Go out for wrestling . . . get all beat up. Mm-*mm*. That boy must have *something*, make a girl do that."

I kicked her in the shins. She danced away, laughing.

She frosted me the rest of the way home, but she kept her distance.

As I was climbing my steps and they were heading off, she called, good and loud so I could hear: "Tell you one thing, Hamburger, just between you and me. I *hope* she's not doing it 'cause of a clown. I *hope* she's doing it to be . . . whoa! . . . out-*ray*-jus!"

I knew she herself was doing something outrageous, probably in the middle of the street, but I didn't look.

My parents went wacko when they saw my golf-ball lip. John said, "Hey, guys get fat lips." P.K. begged and begged till I let her touch it.

I didn't try to explain the whole thing. I just told them it was the perils of the sport.

Later, my mother poked her head into my room. "Need to talk to Ellen Lupinski?"

"No," I told her. "I'm okay."

"You don't look okay."

"If you just got beat up ten times in a row, you wouldn't look so hot either."

"No argument there."

I dragged my eyes around to look at her. "Believe it or not, I'm even better than okay. I'm happy."

I don't think she understood. But she believed. "Good," she said, and closed the door.

That night was the first time Bernadette spoke to me. Until then I had done all the talking: complaining, telling her what happened in school, stuff like that. But on this night, even though she didn't open her mouth, she spoke. And even though there was no sound, I heard. (People who get close to their pets will understand.)

"Well," I heard her say, kind of huffily, "I'm glad *you're* happy."

"What's your problem?" I said. (I really was talking.)

"Take a look at the bed."

I looked at the bed. I kept looking. Then I saw. "Oh no!" I yanked my old pal Sidney the green snake off my bedstead and put him in the closet. "Bernie, I'm really sorry. That's been making you nervous all this time, hasn't it?"

"Let's put it this way," she said, obviously relieved, "whenever you were out of the room, things got a little tense around here."

Chapter Twenty-one

I HEARD THE VOICES—tiny, whispery voices, not Bernadette's—but I didn't want to hear them. I wanted them to be a dream.

It was two days after the Nutcracker and the first day of Christmas vacation. We had had practice from nine in the morning till noon. For the first time in my life I wanted vacation to end fast so practices would be shorter.

I had come home, gone upstairs, and died on my bed. Didn't these whisperers know enough to leave a dead body rest in peace?

"Wanna touch it?"

"Can I?"

Were they talking about Bernadette? I hoped so.

"Just a little. You gotta be quiet. Shhhh."

"Right. Shhhhh."

I felt it on my lip, on the fat part, which was still three-quarters of a golf ball. I opened my eyes. A little hand darted away with a gasp. I was staring into a tiny, terrified face. I had never seen this face before.

"Hi, Maisie!" P.K. chirped. "This is my new friend, Tank."

Who named this kid? " 'Lo, Tank."

"I told him he could touch your lip."

"Why didn't you charge him? You could make money."

"Hey!" P.K. shot her hand under Tank's nose. "Gimme a nickel."

Tank shoved her hand away. "Too late. I already felt it."

I liked this kid. He stood up to my sister.

"Tank says boys are stronger than girls. That ain't true, is it, Maisie?"

"It's true," I said.

Her face collapsed. "It *is*?"

"Yeah. Stronger-smelling."

P.K. howled. She shrank away from Tank, holding her nose and going "Ouuuu!"

Tank sniffed his armpits. "I don't smell."

"Check your belly button," I told him.

For the next minute, Tank tried every contortion known to man, trying to bring his nose to his belly button. Finally, he came to the bed, pulled up his shirt, and said with a grim little face, "I can't reach. Will you smell it?"

I cracked up. "Just kidding, Tank." I grabbed him, rolled him onto the bed with a fireman's carry, and pinned him with a massive tickle to the stomach. He went crazy. Of course, P.K. had to jump in, screaming, "Tickle war!"

I never had a chance. Their hands were smaller than mine, but there were four of them and they were quick. And by the time P.K. was done telling Tank where all my secret tickle spots were, I practically died again, this time from laughing. I was saved by my mother, who heard the racket and chased out the runts.

No sooner did I re-fall asleep than I felt something on my lip again. I opened one eye—and saw a wall of faces.

P.K. had rounded up every kid she could find. They lined up at the bed and one by one they touched the lip. But before they did, they had to drop a nickel in the bathroom glass in P.K.'s hand. She made forty-five cents.

From then on, P.K. and Tank were waiting for me every day after practice. (The coach gave us the day before Christmas and Christmas Day off. Wow-wee.) Sometimes they had contests of strength, like arm wrestling, or how many volumes of the World Book Encyclopedia can you lift?

Sometimes they made me teach them new wrestling holds.

One day they appointed me referee for their Main Event. They both wore bathing suits. I didn't know who looked funnier—Tank, wearing P.K.'s one piece Batman suit or P.K. in her yellow bikini with her Washerwoman's mop, sponge, and pail of soapy water.

They had set up a ring in my room: four chairs for the ringposts and Christmas ribbon for the ropes.

Poor Tank. In a fair fight he would have done okay, but he was no match for Washerwoman. She bopped him with the mop and swabbed him with the sponge. But when she threatened to dump the pail of soapy water on him, I declared the bout a draw and kicked them out.

The next day they were in bathing suits again, but not for wrestling. This time it was bodybuilding.

One thing never changed. Every day they begged me to take them to practice. A couple of days before New Year's, I agreed.

Usually I got up at eight to make the nine o'clock practice. P.K. was bouncing on my bed at seven.

Tank's house was in the next block. He was on the front step, throwing snowballs. When he saw us, he came running.

Along the way, I found out his real name: Rodney. I asked where he got his nickname.

"My daddy," he said. "He says if I have a tough name, I'll grow up to be tough."

Something told me I should be glad I had ten years on this kid.

Against one wall of the wrestling room was the rolled-up mat used for matches with other schools. That's where I parked Tank and P.K.

P.K. didn't stay parked for long. She kept sliding down and challenging guys. She didn't have much luck with the ones in action, but some of the sitters took her on. For P.K., the bigger the better. Her eyes lit up when she spotted Heavy Henry Epps. Every time I looked over, she was pinning him.

Even Mr. Cappelli took a minute with them. He hoisted one in each arm and carried them to the Nutcracker honor roll and showed them my name.

After practice, I had them wait in the hallway while I changed. When I came out, they were both attacking a new target, Eric Delong.

I managed to peel Tank off, but P.K. had Eric's neck in a death grip. Eric didn't seem to mind so I let her be. I was glad my lip was back to normal.

It was the best walk I could ever remember: down the long hallway (but not long enough), Tank holding my hand, P.K. perched on Eric Delong's shoulders, the four of us laughing, saying stuff, P.K. blinding Eric with her hands, Eric smiling that swimming pool smile, Eric saying, "Are you as good as your big sister?"

Then, way too soon, out into the sunlight, eye-squinting, the snow brighter than water, the hockey field dazzling. Down to the sidewalk, Eric saying, "Well, I go that way." P.K. hanging on, clinging, not wanting to let go, pleading. "No, you come with us!"

I couldn't get her off. He had to do it.

On the way home she asked me his name. "Eric," I said. And even though I knew she heard, I said it again. "Eric."

80   THERE'S A GIRL IN MY HAMMERLOCK

And all that day and night I kept hearing him say the words "big sister." And exactly what, I wondered, did he mean by "good"?

By the first day back to school, I was fat. I gaped at the scale before practice: 107! And the first match, against Franklinville, in less than a week.

I thought Mr. Cappelli would blow his top but what he said was "I have a present for you, Potter."

"A present?"

I took my eyes from the scale. He looked pleased with himself.

"Yep. Little present from me to you. I thought you could use a little support from your own kind around here. So I told the girls' gym class teachers I needed another student manager. They made announcements today—"

He looked toward the door. He smiled. He beamed. "Ahhh, this must be her."

I turned to see the equally smiling, beaming face of Her Supreme Lipness, the Lizard of Loveliness, Elizabeth Lampley.

"Thanks," I said.

Chapter Twenty-two

MAT MAID."

That's what Mr. Cappelli called her.

She had a whole slew of other titles and jobs, depending on how you looked at it. To Mr. Cappelli she was Student Medical Assistant and Assistant in Charge of Female Support for Maisie Potter.

The guys had another job for her: Assistant in Charge of Being Gawked At and Slobbered Over. (Kruko said to somebody, making sure it was loud enough for me to hear, "Now, *that's* a girl.")

To Her Exalted Selfness, she was Assistant in Charge of Keeping an Eye on Eric Delong and Screwing Up Maisie Potter Whenever Possible.

She watched him—and me—like a hawk. If we got anywhere near each other, you could see her stiffen. If we were running in the same group, she'd find some reason to be out in the hallway.

Whenever Eric was sitting, she would be there, asking if he was hurt, giving him a fresh towel. Then she'd start toweling him off herself. Or she'd flap the towel in front of him, giving him a nice cool breeze.

i don't mean to say she ignored the other guys. Anybody got hurt, there she was with the medical box, a little white suitcase, setting it on the mat, opening it, waiting for Mr. C. to tell her what to hand over: cotton ball, Band-Aid, hydrogen peroxide. And then she would give the wounded warrior those eyes and that face and you could see the guy getting better right then.

Of course, with me it was a little different. No towels, no fanning. No—I take that back. She did give me a towel once. As I opened it to wipe my face, I saw boogies on it.

Once, while I was wrestling George Bamberger, his fingernail scratched my face. All of a sudden there was Lizard kneeling beside us with her little white suitcase. She pushed George away.

"Hey, what are you doing?" I said.

"I'm fixing you." She opened the case.

"Fixing me? I'm broke?"

"You're bleeding."

She pointed to my cheek. She was right. I touched it and came away with a fingertip of blood.

Then things happened fast. I glanced around for Mr. Cappelli. He was by the door, watching, like, Oh, isn't that nice, taking care of her fellow female. I turned back to Lizard. "I'll fix my—" and then the cotton ball was on my cheek, drenched with hydrogen peroxide, gouging, digging at the scratch, burning it, like touching a hot stove, the purple-painted lizard eyes gleaming. I yelled, I jerked away. I grabbed some dry cotton and cured myself. I didn't want to hurt Mr. Cappelli's feelings. That's the only reason I didn't wallop her.

The next day I regretted that I hadn't. I bumped into the lovers swapping spit between third and fourth periods. I had known that they were a kissy couple by now but I had never actually seen them in action.

I tried to get away clean, but she cooed after me. "Hi, Maisie."

"Hi, Lizard," I said.

I vowed never to pass up another chance to fatten her lip. See how Mr. Delong liked sucking on a golf ball.

As it was, I managed to get my shots in too.

Usually we practiced against people our own weight or close to it. But sometimes, for fun, Mr. Cappelli would call out two weight classes pretty far apart and let them go at it, to see what would happen. When he called out "one-oh-five" and "one-thirty" one day, the Lizard almost dropped her scales.

Eric and I put on a great bout if I do say so myself. Usually he could pin me pretty fast, but I used every trick I knew to keep it going. I even had him in a cradle hold for a couple of seconds. That's where you're both on the mat, and you hook the back of your opponent's knee with one arm and pull up; meanwhile you're hugging him tight around his neck with your other arm. You bring your own hands together, making a hoop of your arms, and squeeze to bend him so his knee and chin come together. Then you rock him back—like a cradle—onto his shoulders. I couldn't hold it enough for a pin, but we were a pretty cozy number while it lasted. Then Eric was shooting holds on me that Lizard would probably kill for. I snuck looks at her whenever I could.

She was on her knees, creeping across the mat, her eyes wild, a towel clenched in her teeth. To top it off, when it ended I gave him a pat on the butt, like any good teammate would. Her ears were smoking.

Then we practiced a different kind of thing. For a real match here's the way it goes. The team comes trotting out of the locker room and into the gym single file. You trot into a circle on the mat with the captain in the middle. The captain leads you in calisthenics. Then everybody splits into pairs and you do some easy, slow-motion moves with each other.

It's all just to loosen up. For show. The important thing is to make sure you're scowling the whole time. So if your opponent on the other team is watching, maybe he'll get scared.

Then comes the *really* important part: the pile-on. The captain gives a signal and everybody dives headfirst to the middle of the mat. In a couple of seconds you've got a human sandwich about five feet high. You shout three times, real fierce—"RAVENS! RAVENS! RAVENS!"—and then you unpile and run to your seats, punching your fists in the air and scowling worse than ever and yelling "Yeah! Yeah!" or whatever, because you're a pack of crazed psycho mad dogs now and God help anybody dumb enough to wrestle you.

So for the benefit of the rookies, and I guess to get the whole team pumped for Franklinville, Mr. Cappelli had us do a dry run entrance on the day before our first match. I did okay until the pile-on. I made the mistake of being one of the first to dive in, which made me the bottom deck on the sandwich, three tons of guys squashing me. The only consolation was knowing how bad Lizard was wishing she were me right then.

Mr. C. had us do the pile-on once more. This time I was smart. I waited till nearly everybody had piled. Then I dove for the top. And that's where I banged into the Lovely One—I knew she couldn't stand it—diving onto the pile from the other side.

Chapter Twenty-three

So, LESS THAN TWENTY-FOUR HOURS LATER, what was I doing wearing my grandmother's bathing suit in a room with two men staring at me?

Good question.

You could say it was my fault for pigging out over the Christmas vacation and ballooning up to 107.

You could say it was the coach's fault for not telling me sooner what happens on match day.

Or you could blame it on the wrestling industry, with its silly rule that if you weigh a zillionth of an ounce more than you're supposed to, zap—you're on the bench.

All Mr. Cappelli had said to me after practice the night before the Franklinville match was "You might want to bring a bathing suit along tomorrow. You're pretty close to not making weight."

He said it as I was heading for the locker room, real casual. He started it off with "Oh, Potter, by the way . . ." Low-key. No big deal. That was usually his approach. You're just one of the guys, Potter. No special treatment. Which was fine with me. That's how I wanted it. So I didn't think too much about what he said. At the moment.

By the time I got home, I was thinking plenty.

The guys, the veterans, had been talking for weeks about making weight. About starving themselves. About standing in hot showers for hours with sweat suits on. And then, the day of the match, not eating a thing. Or maybe just an orange. Weigh-in time getting closer and closer. Don't even drink water. Your body's a one-way street— everything out, nothing in. Go to the bathroom as much as you can. Cut your hair if you have to. Trim you nails. Blow your nose. Clean out your ears, your belly button. Forget your deodorant. Whatever it takes—so when you step on that scale, you're not over.

All I had for dinner was a grapefruit. John sat there grinning and gloating and shoveling about nineteen helpings of meat loaf into his mouth.

I tried on last year's bathing suit. I threw a fit.

My mother didn't even have one to lend me. She had thrown her old one away and was waiting for summer to buy a new one. This was nine o'clock on a weeknight.

"What am I gonna *do?*" I screeched.

"Shorts?" my mother suggested.

I checked them out. Only one pair really fit me from last year, and they were made of heavy material: denim.

I stripped down and stood on the bathroom scale: 105½.

Did my underwear weigh a half-pound? Was the scale accurate?

My mother appeared at the bathroom door. She was holding something. I asked what it was.

"A bathing suit." She said it with a perfectly straight face.

"Right. What is it really? A little kid's clown costume? Halloween?"

It was white with bright red polka dots the size of quarters.

"A bathing suit, really. The only one in the house. It was Grandmom's."

"*Grandmom's!*" I stared at it "What—"

The rest of the sentence—are you doing with it, holding it there in the bathroom doorway in front of me?—never left my mouth. I already knew the horrible answer.

I carried the bathing suit into my room. Bernadette stood up, her little black eyes round as berries. "Don't say a word," I snapped.

So there I was next day in the boys' locker room in my grandmother's red and white polka dot bathing suit. The scale had been moved because of the windows in the coach's office. No privacy. The boys had already been weighed and cleared out. It looked the same as the girls' locker room to me, except for the urinals.

Mr. Cappelli, being the home team coach, did the weighing. The coach from Franklinville watched.

I stepped onto the scale. I kept staring straight ahead. Don't look down, I kept telling myself. You are *not* wearing what you think. You are wearing a gorgeous, expensive, up-to-the-minute bathing suit, maybe even a bikini. I had a sudden panic that my feet were dirty, but I kept my eyes up.

The little weight slid down the bar. The pointer bounced and settled.

"Ooo-kay," said Mr. Cappelli. "Looks like one-oh-five to me."

The Franklinville coach stepped forward. He leaned in. I got a whiff of cologne. He wore a gold necklace. His underwear was probably twice as sexy as my bathing suit. I didn't like him already.

"Looks a tad over to me," he said.

Mr. Cappelli leaned in, squinted. "You're calling it awfully close there."

Mr. Smell Me straightened up. He shrugged. He didn't say anything.

I looked at the pointer. I couldn't believe he was making something of it. "That's not a tad," I said. "That's a tenth of a tad. It's hardly visible."

For the first time he looked at me. "But it *is* visible."

"Yeah," I told him, "and so's my bathing suit, which is my grandmother's, by the way. It weighs a tad. But see, I'm not a *boy*. The boys can stand here in their jockstraps and get weighed. And if *they're* a tad over, they can just take off their jocks." I looked him right in his sweet-smelling face. "Do I have to take off my bathing suit? Huh?"

He stared at me. He sniffed and gave a snide grin.

"Okay," he said, and walked out.

Chapter
Twenty-four

FORTY MINUTES LATER, led by Captain Mike Kruko, we trotted single file into the gym. The place went wild. Cheering, whistling, stomping on the bleachers. "Ra-vens! Ra-vens!" I was surprised the stands were so full. I wondered where my mother and P.K. were sitting. My father said he would try to get out of work. Was he there too? I wished Bernadette could be there. I knew John wasn't.

I didn't look. I trotted into that happy thunder of cheering, pretending I didn't hear it, keeping my eyes fixed on the back of the guy in front of me. We formed our circle, did our exercises, broke into our one-on-one warm-ups. A man was by the mat, taking flash pictures. At one point I caught myself almost smiling and had to quick put my scowl back on.

When Kruko called for the pile-up, his face was blue with fury. He was a demon. For the first time I think I actually liked him. We were a *team*. "All right!" he snarled. "Let's do it!" He pumped his fists. We pumped our fists: "Yeah!" He yelled, "Ravens!" and dived to the middle of the mat. We were on him like nine kids on an eight-slice pizza. "RAVENS! RAVENS! RAVENS!"

Man, in that pile, right then, I loved those guys. My face was buried in body parts. I dropped my scowl. I grinned. I giggled. I felt like crying.

Even more, I felt like wrestling. Or fighting or kicking heads or whatever the poor dumb Franklinville 105-pounder wanted to do.

We lined up along our side of the mat, starting with 70-pound Gary Pompano and ending with Heavy Henry Epps. I scowled across the mat at my 105-pound opponent. I scowled so hard I could feel my face bones creak. It was all I could do to keep from growling. I was a little surprised he didn't blink or look down at the mat or turn and run back to the bus. He just stared, his face like a stone. The others were doing pretty much the same. *Gee*, I thought, *maybe they don't go in for scowling at Franklinville*.

The timer's table was off to another side, in front of the bleachers. A microphone sat in front of the timer, who was actually Mr. Ollnik, the biology teacher. He said:

"Welcome, ladies and gentlemen, to a new season of wrestling! [cheers] Our first match of the year is between Green Hornets of Franklinville [mild applause] and the *RRRRRRavens* of Lenape Valley Junior High School!" [thunder, lightning, tidal wave].

Then the introductions.

"In the seventy-pound class, for Franklinville, Bill Taylor! . . . For Lenape Valley . . . Gary Pompano!"

More cheers. The two of them trotted to the middle of the mat, shake hands, go back.

75 pounds . . . 85 . . .

"At one hundred and five pounds, for Franklinville . . ."

I didn't even catch the kid's name. Harry, I think. Or Hobart. Whatever. All I heard was ". . . Maisie Potter!"

Out of the noise came a squeaky voice: "Go, Maisie!"

P.K. was there all right.

I was so anxious, I practically long-jumped to the middle of the mat. For a couple of seconds, the kid didn't move. I figured my scowl was working. Finally he lumbered forward. His face wasn't so stony now. He was blinking, twitching. His eyes were landing everywhere but on me. All *right*, I thought, this bozo's scared to death of me. I stuck out my hand. I was going to give him a good hard shake, but as soon as my fingers touched his, he pulled away. It was like trying to shake hands with a fish. Flashbulbs went off.

I trotted back, thinking, This kid is *mine*.

Gary Pompano lost his 70-pound bout. He got pinned with a cradle hold with only twenty seconds left. The noise was deafening.

Even though he lost, Gary got a hand as he came off the mat. We all lined up and patted him on the back and said way to go. "You're always a winner when you're a Raven," says Mr. Cappelli.

Gary Pompano wasn't too impressed by all that. As he left the mat, he ripped his headgear and slammed it to the floor. Mr. C. waited for him at the end of our pat-on-the-back line. Mr. C. shook him, told him, "Never do that again. It's bush. You lose, you take it like a man."

Of the seven bouts before mine, we won four and lost three. Win or lose, each one was exciting. But the best part was something I hadn't even known about.

Here's how it goes. You sit in your chair until two or three bouts before yours. Then you go behind the chairs and go through your own little routine to prime yourself for your bout—jog in place, roll your neck, punch the wall, whatever works for you. You think about what you're going to do to your opponent. Shut everything else out. Your brain grows claws, digs in, until your bout is the only thing you know.

Then it happens. The bout before yours ends. Up till now, Mr. Cappelli has been with the team on the chairs. In front of them, actually, on his knees, going crazy, yelling instructions, shooting moves on Mr. Paul to show the kid on the mat what to do. But now, with the bout over, he comes back to you.

He takes your face in his hands, and it's just you and him, and he goes, "You can do it" or "You ready to have fun?" Something like that. And then he stands behind you, real close. You fold your arms over your chest and hold them real stiff. His arms come around, wrapping you, cupping your elbows. Then he pulls you even closer to himself, your back to his chest, and then you're off your feet, because he's lifting you, he's lifting you and bouncing you in the air, whether you're 70 or 200 pounds. It's one final exercise to stretch your bones, shake you loose, get you ready. But it's more. It's you and your coach. It's your coach lifting you up.

From my chair, each time a bout ended, I turned around to watch. Then the 95-pound bout began. I got up, went to the back. As I loosened up, I tried to focus on my bout but all I could think of was the coach lifting and bouncing me.

I looked across the way for my opponent. He was still sitting. He sat through the 95-pound bout. The 100-pounders came on and he was still sitting. I couldn't believe it.

The 100-pound bout ended. His coach was kneeling in front of him, talking to him. Mr. Cappelli was coming back to me. He kept looking across the way. He wasn't happy. When he got to me, he didn't put my face in his hands. He didn't say, "You can do it." He said, "I was afraid of this."

Coach Smell Me was walking to the timer's table.

Mr. Ollnik was saying, "In the one-hundred-five-pound class, we have a forfeit. The winner, from Lenape . . . Maisie Potter."

I stood there gawking up at Mr. Cappelli.

"Go ahead," he said.

"Go where?"

He pointed to the center of the mat where the referee stood. "There." He slapped me on the rump. "Go."

I trotted out to the referee. He grabbed my wrist and hoisted my hand over my head. Flashbulbs popped. Somewhere in the noise, P.K. was shrieking, "The winner! The winner!"

As I left the mat, Mr. Cappelli was lifting the 110-pounder.

Chapter Twenty-five

    I guess it's pretty obvious by now,
Mr. or Ms. Editor. This letter to you
has gotten a little out of hand.

    I mean, a letter with chapters?

    I guess it's become a Book to the
Editor.

    As you will see, it's about to become
a Scrapbook to the Editor. I'm going to
be pasting some clippings from *The
Evening Post* to go along with my words.

    I guess I'm thinking of you now
because this is where you—or at least
your newspaper—enters the picture. Some
of the clippings I got from other
people. It never occurred to me at the
time that I would ever want to see that
stuff again.

    I guess this letter isn't just to you
anymore. It's also a Letter to Myself.

    So, to continue . . .

As SOON AS I GOT HOME NEXT DAY, P.K. came screaming
"Maisie! You're famous! You're famous!"

She was waving *The Evening Post* at me. When I finally got it from
her, I saw it was the sports section, and sure enough, there I was, in
this huge picture that took up a quarter of the page. The one showing
me and Beans Agway in the pre-match warm-up. The one with the
headline:

THERE'S A **GIRL** IN MY HAMMERLOCK!

Which was totally dumb. (I'm sorry if that hurts your feelings or your reporter's.) Because what he was doing was taking me down with an easy, slow motion fireman's carry. I had to admit, Beans did look surprised. But it wasn't from finding a girl slung over him. It was from looking up and finding that stupid camera in his face.

I read the two articles. The one about the whole match and the one about me. I think the one about me is worth pasting in here:

LENAPE VALLEY—History of a sort happened here yesterday when an eighth-grade girl became the first member of her sex to appear with the Lenape Valley Junior High School wrestling team.

And she won.

The victory for Maisie Kay Potter, 13, did not come by way of competition, however. She was awarded a forfeit, worth six points to the team, because her scheduled 105-pound opponent from Franklinville Junior High refused to take the mat against her.

"I ain't wrestling no girl" was the terse comment of Green Hornet eighth-grader Harold Stith.

Comments from Potter herself and her teammates could not be obtained, as Raven coach Vince Cappelli directed that no member of the team be interviewed.

Cappelli himself offered only the following statement: "Miss Potter is the best 105-pound wrestler we have. It's as simple as that."

Observations were easier to come by from the crowd. Estimated at 200, they gave a mixture of reactions.

Said one eighth-grade boy: "She ought to go out for some girl stuff. She don't belong there."

A ninth-grade boy said, with a chuckle, "I hope she's not looking for too many dates. Guys'd be afraid she'd squash 'em."

One eighth-grade girl shrugged: "Hey, different strokes."

While another had a more forceful opinion: "She's weird."

Most faculty members declined to comment.

One teacher, a female, said, "I wish I'd had the nerve when I was her age."

The mother of one of the other Raven wrestlers shook her head. "I don't get it," she said. Her husband answered without words, giving the "thumbs down" sign.

Potter's parents, both of whom were in attendance, replied "No comment" when asked about their daughter. An unidentified little girl accompanying them called, "I have a comment! I have a comment!" as she was picked up and carried from the gym.

Last year Maisie Potter was named "Outstanding Seventh Grade Female Athlete" at Lenape Valley.

At the next match, against West Ridge, the stands were packed. When I was introduced, I got twice as much noise as anybody else. But it wasn't all good. Some was booing. And laughing. I think I even got my first-ever wolf whistle. I couldn't hear P.K.

This time there wasn't even anyone to meet me in the middle of the mat. West Ridge forfeited right off the bat. Once again, no bout, no lift-and-bounce from Mr. C. I never had to leave my seat.

I tried to cheer our guys on but my heart wasn't in it. Except when Eric's turn came. He pinned his man in the second period with a crossface cradle. I jumped up with everyone else and got in line to greet him as he came off the mat. Everybody high-fived him till he got to the end. That's where a new member of the greeting line was waiting: Lizard Liz. She threw her arms around him and shot a liplock on him right there.

It was after this match that I saw the first Letters to the Editor in *The Evening Post*.

> Dear Editor—or should I say Dear Trash Man:
> When I opened your so-called newspaper to the sports page yesterday and saw that picture of a male and female wrestling, I thought I must have brought *Playboy* magazine by mistake. That's where that trash belongs. I thought you were a good clean family newspaper but your just as smutty as them others. From now on I am buying *USA Today*.
>
> A Former Customer

And this letter:

> Is this a joke? Are my school tax dollars really going to girl wrestlers? What's next? Are they going to fill the gym with mud and have all the boys and girls mud wrestle at once? Or maybe have the boys take off their shirts and put on little bow ties and dance around like those Chippydales or whatever they're called?

Are they running a school up there or a brothel? Let's get the State Department of Education off their fannies and find out. I demand an investigation!

And this one:

Obviously the girl is oversexed. I recommend a diet of saltpeter and three cold showers a day.

If that doesn't work, send her to a girls' school somewhere in Tibet. Or better yet, in the immortal words of Hamlet: "Get thee to a nunnery."

I didn't read these things in our own copy of the paper. My parents were hiding it from me. I found them in my locker at school, where some concerned fellow students had slipped them.

One morning when I got to school, there was a pink-dyed jock-strap hanging from my combination lock. Another day I found a note, unsigned, in one of my books. It started: "How does it feel having guys' hands all over you? Maybe you'd like . . ." It was all downhill from there.

For what it's worth, I never really felt hands on me—in practice or later in matches. I mean, not the way that note said and most of the school probably was thinking. I was too busy trying to win, trying to get out of a hold or put one on, trying to *wrestle*.

One day in practice, as George Bamberger and I were grappling on the mat, his hand dragged across my chest. "Sorry," he whispered, and backed off for a second. It was all the opening I needed to shoot a cradle on him for a quick pin. "You're also stupid," I told him. He was never stupid again.

One final thing on this subject: if you've ever seen me, you know there's not much there to feel anyway. I mean, I guess there will be someday; my mother has a pretty good shape. But for now, well, let me put it this way: if I were a vertical cliff and you were sliding down me to your death, there wouldn't be anything sticking out enough for you to grab hold of and save yourself.

Our next match was at Bridgeton. I figured, being away, it would be different.

It wasn't.

Packed gymnasium. Noise. Hoots. Whistles. And this was *before* I was announced.

"You're famous," Beans Agway whispered as we stood in line for introductions.

"I'm ticked," I said.

Once again the announcer used that word I was coming to hate: "forfeit."

I stared across the mat at the 105-pound wimp who wouldn't wrestle me and at his coach. I took a step forward. I yelled, "What's the matter? You chicken?"

The 105-pound wimp was standing there with his hands hanging down and crossed in front of himself, like I was going to attack his crotch or something. His eyes were shifting.

The announcer was silent at the microphone.

I took another step. I pointed. "You afraid of losing to a *girl*? Huh? You afraid I'll beat you and everybody'll laugh at you? You afraid—"

And then Mr. Cappelli was dragging me back, saying things to me, his voice mad, but I could tell, mad at more than just me. He plunked me into my chair. "Sit," he growled, "and shut up."

On the bus on the way home, he said to me, "I'm suspending you for the next match."

"You *can't*," I told him. "I'm undefeated. I'm a guaranteed six points."

His finger was in my face. "Don't get smart, girl, or I'll drop you altogether. I'd never let anybody else get away with a stunt like that and I won't let you either. Any talking to do, I'll do it. You do the wrestling."

I practically screamed: "That's what I'm trying to do!"

The next night, the headline in *The Evening Post* said:

RAVEN CALLS
FOE "CHICKEN"

Chapter Twenty-six

I WAS HALFWAY THROUGH the article when the doorbell rang. I answered it and looked up into the beaming, laughing face of Tina McIntire. Next thing I knew, her long arms were reeling me in and mashing me against her. My nose was somewhere in her chest.

She pushed me to arm's length. She held me by the shoulders. She wagged her head. "*Chicken?*" She cackled and mauled me some more. "You're too much, Maypot." She looked over my head. "Am I coming in or what?"

"Oh yeah, sorry," I ushered her into the house.

Tina went straight for my mother.

"Mrs. Potter, that daughter of yours, I don't know. Calling people *chicken?* What's she gonna call them next?" She draped her arm over my mother's shoulder. She wagged her head in fake dismay. "You sure you're bringing that girl up right?"

My mother gave the same wag. "Sometimes I wonder."

They both laughed.

Tina called over to me, "Well, you going like that?"

"Like what?" I said. "Going where?"

"The dance."

It was Friday, night of the once-a-month dance at school. I'd never been to any of them.

"Who said I'm going to the dance?"

Silly question. Tina didn't even bother to answer. "Tell you one thing, you're not going like this. Scare all the chickens away. Where's your room?"

I led her to my room. Tina stopped at the doorway. "What's that?"

"Meet Bernadette."

"A *rat?*"

"A hooded rat."

She went over. Bernadette stood on her toes and looked up. Tina looked down. She nodded. "Cool." She turned to me. "Now, where's your makeup?"

"I don't have any."

She shrieked. "*What?* You got a rat in your room but no makeup?"

"I use my mom's if I have to. Not that I ever have to."

"Where's your mom's?"

"Bathroom."

Into the bathroom we go.

"Tina," I told her, "I don't *want* makeup."

She grinned and gave me a sly singsong: "You want Errr-ic, don't you?"

I glared at her. She knew I was remembering her words to George Bamberger: "I hope she's not doing it 'cause of a clown."

"Hey, Potter," she said, "it's your life. I'm just here to help out. Besides, if he's a clown, the sooner you find out the better."

I shrugged. "Won't make any difference."

"Why, because the Lizard'll be crawling all over him?"

I screeched. "*You* call her that too?"

We cracked up.

Not long before, my mother had thrown out half her makeup. What little was left, Tina fished through. She did some blush and eye-brow pencil. She was framing my face in her fingers, debating which eye shadow color to use, when P.K. came in. She started staring at Tina's feet and didn't stop till she was gawking straight up.

"Wow," she went. "You're big . . . and you're brown."

"P.K.!" I smacked her hand.

Tina snatched her up and hoisted her face-to-face. P.K. traced her fingertips around one of Tina's cheeks, down her chin, and over to the other cheek. "Wow," she said. "Can I be brown?"

Tina kissed her on the nose. "Maybe if you're lucky someday. But you gotta eat lots of graham crackers."

"What's your name?" said P.K.

Tina went into a southern accent. "Y'all kin call me Tall. What's yours?"

"P.K."

Tina put her back down. "Not anymore. Now your name is . . . Small. You and me, baby. Tall . . . and Small." She held out her hand. P.K. slapped it.

"And this is my friend Tank," said P.K.

She dragged Tank in.

Tina held out her hand. "Tank, my man."

Tank just gawked. Tina took his hand and slapped her own with it.

"Tank's my *best* friend," P.K. told her audience. "He's sleeping over tonight. His mommy said it's okay. His daddy doesn't be home much. His daddy drives a truck, and guess what?"

Tina was wide-eyed and breathless. "What?"

"The truck is bigger than Tank's *house.* Can you *'magine?*"

"What a truck!"

"And Tank's gonna have real big muscles, 'cause his daddy makes him lift barbells. Right, Tank?"

Tank nodded.

"But he don't have big muscles yet 'cause he's still a little boy. I can beat him up whenever I feel like it. Right, Tank?" She looked up at us. "You wanna see me beat him up?"

"No, that's okay," we said. Our teeth were practically biting through our lips, trying not to laugh.

Since that first day I met Tank, when he refused to pay P.K. for touching my golfball lip, P.K. had gotten the upperhand. Not surprising. She and Tina were two of a kind.

"Someday Tank is gonna be big and brave," she was saying, "but right now he's afraid of a lotta stuff." She put her arm around him. "Don't worry, Tank. Pretty soon you'll be *aaall* big, and *you* can beat *me* up." She looked up at Tina. "When girls grow up they lose their muscles and they can't beat up boys anymore."

Tank whispered in her ear. She snapped at him. "*I* know that. I was just gonna *say* it." She turned back to Tina: "Excep' Washerwoman."

Tank whispered to her again.

"I *know.* And my sister. My big sister can beat up *anybody.*" She waved her finger up at Tina. She scowled. "So don't you mess with her or you'll get hurt."

She made Tina promise not to mess with me, before dragging Tank from the bathroom.

Tina finished my makeup. I couldn't decide how I felt about it. For one thing, it wasn't me. For another, I kept thinking of the fool I had already made of myself by losing the H-I-P-P-O game on purpose.

But then—looking at it Tina's way—should I throw away a chance with Eric because of a little lipstick and eye shadow?

I decided I was glad Tina was deciding for me.

We went back to my room then and Tina decked me out in a dress. My only pure dress. A blue and white thing I once wore to my cousin Maureen's wedding. I was saving it in case I ever got invited to the White House.

Looking in the mirror, I had to admit, whoever that person was, she didn't look too bad.

"Walk," said Tina.

I walked across the room. I tried to wiggle a little, like Holly had shown me.

"Oo-*wee*!" Tina hooted. "Dudes, here she comes. Eric Delong, look out."

John stuck his head in the doorway. "A *dress*? What happened to my brother?"

"You're just sorry she's *your* sister," said Tina. "If she wasn't you'd be chasing her all over."

"Yeah," snickered John, "trying to get a leash on her."

When we left the house, Tina and P.K. called:

"Bye, Small."

"Bye, Tall."

Chapter Twenty-seven

I SHOULD HAVE STAYED HOME.

I mean, I only went in the first place because Tina made me. And once I got there, that didn't mean I wanted to dance. Which I didn't want. (Well, okay—a couple times my toes got a little carried away and started to boogie.) I never danced once in my life, not that kind of dance, anyway. (Except with my uncle Harry at Cousin Maureen's wedding, and he made me.) Besides, half the kids at a dance don't dance, anyway.

That's not what I'm saying.

I'm saying, since I was already kidnapped and dragged to school. And since I had to be there from seven-thirty till ten—two and a half hours (because once you're in they don't let you out). And since I *was* all dressed up (even if it wasn't my idea). And since there *was* music, and it *was* a dance (even if half the people didn't dance), well, all I'm saying is, maybe at least I could have been *asked*.

Oh sure, it you want to get technical, you could say I was asked. You could say, What about George Bamberger and Beans Agway? *They* asked you. *They* danced with you.

Right. And wasn't it funny that they just happened to ask me after I saw them having a little chat with a certain six-foot center on the girls' basketball team?

And what about all the times you danced with Tina herself? *She* asked you.

Yeah, right.

I'm just saying, there's asked, and there's *really* asked.

And there are some things that even Tall Tina McIntire can't make happen.

Whether my feet were standing or dancing, my eyes almost never left Eric and Lizard. If I didn't know better, I would have thought they were Siamese twins joined at the navel. The only time I saw them not glued together was when he went to the boys' room. And then she waited right outside for him.

I tried not to look at them. I tried not to feel anything.

When slow dances were on, Lizard would steer him over toward me. She would wrap both arms around his neck. She'd slide one hand under his shirt collar. The fingers of her other hand would slither like little red snakes into the hair on the back of his head. She would close her eyes and make "oo-oo" shapes with her lips. She would bite his earlobe and stick her tongue inside his ear. He would do the same to her. By the time the night was over, they must have had the cleanest ears in the world.

At about the halfway point, Tina came running. She squeezed my arm. "Girls' choice coming up. Ask him."

"You're crazy," I told her.

"*Do* it."

"*She's* there."

"She won't be."

She wasn't.

Just before the girls' choice started, I saw Tina talking with the Lizard. Then they both headed for the girls' room.

"Girls' choice!" came the announcement.

I couldn't believe it. There he was, unattached.

No way was I going to walk over there and ask him to dance.

And I didn't.

Not the real me, anyway.

The girl in the makeup and blue and white dress—the girl under orders from Tina McIntire to *do* it—she's the one who went and did it. Who walked up to him and said, "Hi, Eric. Want to dance?"

She's the one he looked at and looked away from and looked back at. She's the one he was thinking about right then, almost smiling that swimming pool smile, getting ready to say something, turning to answer . . .

But she wasn't the one left standing there like a jerk when Lizard Liz came charging across the floor, practically tackling him and dragging him away.

No, that was me.

Standing there because I didn't know how to move. I mean, when you've been blown away like that—*erased*—how do you move? Where do you go?

Eventually I went to the girls' room, stayed there a long time in a daze. Later, I remember waves of boys breaking away from me, turning and fading. They made a chickenish sound—"Bawlllk ba-bawlllk!"— to warn each other that I was coming. They actually seemed to believe I might ask them to dance.

Tina kept gabbing at me, trying to make me feel better. The clincher came toward the end of the dance. All night long some girls had been taking a poll. I didn't even know what it was about. Nobody polled me, and I didn't ask. About nine forty-five, with fifteen minutes left to go, squeals rang out from the gaggle of pollsters, and they ran to tape a piece of paper to the entrance door. Just about then I started hearing, beyond Tina's louder and louder voice, other voices giggling, "Congratulations."

I headed for the door. Tina tried to stop me. I pushed her away. The lettering on the paper was big and black, from a thick felt-tip marker. It said:

> HUNKIEST BOY AT THE DANCE
> Winner—Eric Delong
> Runner-up—Maisie Potter

P.K.'s room was dark and the door almost shut as I walked past it that night, so I was surprised to hear a voice. "Hi, Maisie."

I went in. P.K. was zonked. "Tank," I whispered. "What are you doing awake?"

"I don't know," he said.

"Well, time to sleep now. Good night."

I was bending over to tuck him in when suddenly he was squeezing me, clinging to me. I waited. He hung on. I lifted him from the bed. I kissed him. "You okay there, partner?"

"Am now," he giggled. He kissed me back and scrambled under the covers.

Chapter Twenty-eight

AT LAST SOMEBODY WRESTLED ME.

I lost.

It was against Hamilton, at home. (Coach didn't suspend me.) I found out early on, during the weigh-in. I was standing on the scale in my new one-piece ultra-lightweight bathing suit, and I asked the Hamilton coach right out: "You going to forfeit too?"

He lifted his eyes from the scale. He grinned. "Hey—we're no chickens."

"All *right!*" I said. I grabbed his hand and pumped it.

The gym sounded like a barnyard when I trotted to center mat for the introductions. It absolutely exploded when the Hamilton 105-pounder trotted out with his headgear in his hand.

His name was Frank somebody. He gave me an all-world scowl. For a split second I wanted to run and hide, but I recovered. We didn't shake hands—we yanked them. Frank from Hamilton hated me. He was pumped. I think he even growled at me. I thought, *Great.*

I didn't know which I felt better about: that I was finally going to wrestle or that I was finally going to get the lift-and-bounce from the coach.

It was just like I knew it would be, maybe better.

As soon as the 100-pound bout ended, Mr. Cappelli came over to me. He took my face in his hands. He brought his face closer and closer. His eyes were brown. They looked into my eyes. They looked into *me.* And then they were so close they were out of focus.

He said, "Well, here we go."

I said, "Yep."

"What you've been waiting for."

"Yeah."

"Maisie?"

"Huh?"

"You can do it."

As he said it, he stepped back and gave my face a little slap. Then he was behind me, lifting me. He lifted me so easy, I thought he might toss me up to the ceiling. *He called me Maisie!* I thought I might fly. His arms were tight around me. They made me want to stay, not to go out into that bright, wild barnyard where they were shrieking, "BAWLLLK! Ba-ba-BAWLLLLK ba-BAWLLLLLLK!" But even more, they made me want to do good for him. As I bounced, my feet never touching the floor, it was like a crust shook loose from me.

I was *ready*.

"Go!" he said.

I hit the floor running. I charged onto the mat . . .

And got pinned in twenty-two seconds flat.

Frank from Hamilton didn't mess around. No circle, circle, shuffle shuffle for him. The instant the ref blew the whistle, Frank dove at my legs. I was quick enough to get one out of the way, but one was all he needed. He gave it a twist and I fell flat on my face. I shot to one side. He was there, like a ton on top of me. He had my legs pretzeled with his. He had my left wrist, so my left arm couldn't go where it wanted. His chin was grinding a hole in the back of my neck, and he was taking my right shoulder someplace it had never been before.

He shifted. Ah—an opening, the pressure suddenly gone on my right. I moved into it. I could feel him give. I pushed, I rolled—now *he* was on the bottom, I had—no—we were still rolling—now it was me on the bottom. We stopped rolling. I was locked. Flat between him and the mat.

Thump!

The referee's hand came down so hard, my head took a little hop off the mat.

I got up. The ref hoisted Frank's arm.

We shook hands. He didn't hate me now. I told him, "Good going." He said, "You too." He turned to his teammates and threw his fists in the air. They swallowed him up, jumping and yelling.

"Good going!" I called to them all.

Right then, all the things I felt were good.

I felt good that I had wrestled. Not just in practice. No forfeit.

In a weird kind of way, I felt good about losing. I mean, it wasn't a totally negative thing. It wasn't empty, like a win by forfeit. I worked for that defeat. I earned it. It was *mine*.

I felt good because the Hamilton team thought that a victory over me was worth celebrating.

And I even felt good for Frank, that it made him so happy.

I didn't really tune in on the crowd until I headed back to our side. The stands were going crazy, whistling, cheering. The Ravens were waiting. I felt them patting me. "Nice try . . . nice try . . ."

But something was wrong. Inside out.

I got back to my chair. I sat down.

The cheering was still going on.

That was it.

We were home. These were the home team fans. Raven fans. This was for-the-winner cheering. Even though the Raven got pinned. They were happy I lost. I didn't feel so good anymore.

"It wasn't everybody," my mother said later. "It was just a couple of nitwits and hard-core chauvinists glad to see a girl lose, that's all."

"I was okay till I heard all that," I said. "I didn't really mind getting pinned."

"You made a rookie mistake," my father said.

"Yeah, that's right. He suckered me, and I went for it. Mr. Cappelli said he's a ninth-grader. One of the best around."

"You did well to last that long with him," my mother said. "You should be proud."

"I'm trying to be."

My father said, "Back in the principal's office, you said you didn't care—"

I snapped out. "They won't *let* me not care!"

"Your coach tried to tell—"

"So *what?*" I yelled. "Nobody said anything about being voted Number Two Hunk in the school. Nobody said anything about chickens bawlking around you all day long. Nobody said my own crowd would cheer the other kid for beating me." I pointed at my father. "You're always so big on being fair. Well, this ain't fair!" The tears were coming. "And it ain't easy!"

"We know," my mother called as I ran up to my room.

I slammed the door shut. Bernadette was standing. "It ain't easy!" I screeched at her.

"Hey," she said, "don't holler at me. I'm your rat, not your mother. I have problems of my own."

"Yeah," I said "like what?" You don't have to worry about snakes or cats or mousetraps. You don't have to go scrounging around dirty dumps and alleys for food, like other rats. You live like a queen."

"Yeah," she said sarcastically, "a fat queen. Look at this potbelly I'm getting. You know why? Because I don't get enough exercise, that's why. I'm cooped up in here all day. Why do you think I'm standing wanting to get out?"

I put her on my bed. She scampered around for a minute, then climbed onto my lap and looked up at me. "I'm hungry."

I gave her a raisin. She loves raisins. In her tiny mouth it looked big as a prune. She hunched on the pillow and nibbled away at it. At least one person in the room was happy.

P.K. knocked on the door and called, "Maisie, Mommy said I had to knock on your door and not barge in 'cause you're out of sorts. Does that mean you're grouchy, Maisie?"

"Yes."

"Are you crying?"

"None of your business."

I heard my mother pulling her away, and P.K. calling, "Don't cry, Maisie! Washerwoman is coming!"

She wasn't kidding.

For the next match she showed up with her pail and mop. What made it even more impressive, the match was away, at T.D. Cooney.

We ran out for the warm-ups, and there was P.K., up in the bleachers, surrounded by the enemy, yelling and waving the mop. I had a hard time keeping my scowl on.

For the second match in a row, I had an opponent. Cory somebody. I had two main goals: I wasn't going to roll myself into a pin, and I was going to last more than twenty-two seconds.

My chances looked good. The coach told me this Cory kid was a seventh-grader. He was a pretty scrawny-looking 105. When we shook hands, he looked like he wanted to be anyplace but in that gym.

I should have known. He wasn't as bad as he looked. He got a takedown on me right after the whistle. But he couldn't control me like Frank of Hamilton. I had room. I used it. I used my speed and squirminess. "Show him the lights, Slime!" my teammates called. I could hear Mr. Cappelli shouting, "Explode! . . . Explode!" But when I saw my opening, I didn't explode. I squirted.

I was free!

The ref raised his hand, one finger up: escape.

My first-ever escape! My first-ever *point*.

I glanced at the scoreboard. I was losing 2 to 1. What a beautiful score!

And the time: thirty seconds were gone.

I had done it!

While I was busy congratulating myself, Cory was tackling me for another takedown. We grunted and grappled around the mat. We were close. Too close. I could smell the hoagie he had for lunch. I had to get away from that smell. I managed to grab his knee. I started to pull myself away from his breath. That's when I heard P.K.'s voice:

"Washerwoman! Washerwoman!"

It was so loud, I couldn't believe she was up in the stands.

She wasn't.

I saw mop strings flying.

I heard Cory of T.D. Cooney spluttering.

I heard the referee's whistle.

I heard P.K. yelling, "Mop of Death! . . . Mop of Death!" as she swished and swabbed the mop in Cory's face. The bucket was on her head.

The ref picked up P.K.

P.K. mopped the ref's face.

The ref handed P.K. to my mother, who was at the edge of the mat. The last time I had seen that look on my mother's face, I was five years old and I had just dumped my birthday cake on my brother John's head.

My mother hauled P.K. back to their seats to a standing ovation.

The ref talked to the timer's table, the bout was restarted with twenty-nine seconds left in the first period, and I got shown the lights with three of those seconds still on the clock.

Chapter Twenty-nine

OF COURSE, *The Evening Post* ate it up.

"WASHERWOMAN" MOPS UP
BIG SISTER'S OPPONENT

Then the parents jumped in.

PTA GOES FOR PIN
ON GIRL GRAPPLER

I had to admit, the headlines were clever. It was those six mothers I wasn't too crazy about, writing that letter to the principal, telling him I was corrupting the student body, and the wrestling season was becoming a sideshow (a word Mr. Cappelli had used).

Of course, I just loved the minister who gave the sermon about how things were getting out of hand, one of his examples being "a girl who wrestles boys right here in our own town."

And of course, there were the ever-popular Letters to you, Mr. or Ms. Editor:

> Since prehistoric times the female of the species has been the caretaker of home and hearth. She is made for nurturing, not combat.

> What will she tell her children when she grows up?

> Lock her in the kitchen where she belongs.

During this stretch I won two bouts—by forfeit. The others I lost by first period pins.

Every time Mr. Cappelli gave me the lift-and-bounce, I told him I'd do better. He said my best was good enough.

Once when I got pinned, a whole bunch of safety pins came raining down on the mat. The principal made an announcement the next day, saying knock it off, but from then on I could always count on one or two pins plunking me from the stands. If a pin happened to land near the Madonna of Medicine, she would lob it over and smirk, "This must be for you."

Another time, while I was warming up, something white landed at my feet. I picked it up. It was a diaper.

It got to the point where the only time I was really happy was during the actual bouts. Which meant about two minutes a week. Out there on the mat, between the ref's starting whistle and the thump of his hand, I was safe. I guess that's why I was mad that I could never last longer than the first period.

And then, against Upper Jonesford, I did.

The kid had me in three near falls, but I squirmed out each time. "Go, Slime!" my teammates were yelling. I scored on two escapes and a reversal, then got my first-ever takedown. The buzzer sounded— first time a first period of mine didn't end in a *thump!*

I jumped up, itching for the next period. I was ecstatic—until thirty seconds into the second period, when he pinned me. While the Ravens slapped me on the back, kids in the stands were chanting, "Potter, Potter, she's our man!"

And I knew that the laughing I heard was over the joke going around school that day:

"When is a swimmer like somebody wrestling Maisie Potter?"
"When?"
"When he's doing the *breast stroke!*"

Give my mother credit, she tried. She kept being chatty and jolly around me. She even suggested I write a Letter to the Editor myself. I sneered, "Why would I want to do a dumb thing like that?" (Little did I know.)

One night Ellen Lupinski appeared at my bedroom door with her scarf and overnight bag. I talked to her and let her stay, because I didn't want to hurt her feelings. But her visit just didn't do much good this time.

Bernadette tried too. She would stand on the salt wheel and reach to the top of the tank. She would pirouette on her hind legs. She would say, "Hey, come on, I'm being as cute as I can. Lighten up."

I would come home from a match, put Bernadette on my desk, flump into my chair.

"A rat's life, huh?" she would say.

"The bout was great," I would say. "It's all the other stuff."

"Tell me about it."

I'd tell her about it, for an hour, maybe more. Sometimes I'd cry. With Bernadette I could always cry. A million times I said, "It's not the wrestling, it's the *people*."

"Tell me about it."

And then one day in early February, in the locker room before practice, Tall Tina pulled me into a corner and whispered, "They broke up."

"Who's they?" I said.

Her eyes were bright and her grin was wicked. "Who do you *think?*"

Chapter Thirty

I GUESS TINA WAS RIGHT, because Lizard didn't show up at practice that day. Good thing we didn't have a medical emergency.

Eric looked glum. Either he had girl trouble or a bad case of jock itch.

I didn't saying anything to him. He didn't say anything to anybody.

Not only did I not talk to him, I didn't even look at him. When I caught myself thinking about him, I stopped. I don't know why. I felt nervous, even scared maybe. I don't know what of.

It was pretty much the same next day. By now the whole school knew.

After practice that night, I left with George, Beans, and some of the other guys. The walkways were shoveled, but snow was a foot deep everywhere else. Heavy Henry Epps decided to be funny. He picked me up—me screaming and punching his head—walked ten giant steps into the snow, plunked me down, and went back to the walkway.

This was great fun to him because he had lumberjack boots on, but I was wearing flimsy flats. My ankles were packed in show. It was already inside my shoes.

"Get back here, lardbutt!" I yelled. "Come get me!"

I couldn't go back in his boot holes because he had taken such long strides.

"Somebody!" I hollered.

Everybody stood there laughing.

"You go."

"No, *you* go."

Eric came out, by himself.

"Hey, Longo, *you* go get her!"

Eric barely dragged his gloomy eyeballs in my direction, dragged them back, and kept on walking.

At long last Bamberger and Agway rescued me. They each grabbed an armpit, lifted, and hauled me out. By then, Eric was out to the street and halfway down the block.

So it's no wonder I was shocked when I picked up the phone that night and heard his voice saying "Want to go out Friday?"

A couple of years passed before I answered. When I did, I croaked, "I have school Friday."

Brilliant, huh?

"I mean Friday night," he said.

Another year.

"Okay," I said.

"Okay," he said.

He hung up.

I realized the phone was still in my hand when I heard that machine gun honking sound. I hung up.

Friday was tomorrow.

For once I didn't know what to say to Bernadette. Just as well. I wouldn't have made much sense.

I tried to do some homework, but math and Spanish looked pretty much the same to me. I went to brush my teeth and squirted enough Aqua-fresh for ten toothbrushes.

I wasn't fit for anything but going to bed, which I did. As near as I could figure from the big red numbers on my digital clock, I fell asleep sometime after 3:15 A.M. and woke up at 5:23.

I never tasted my breakfast. As I left for school, Bernadette was standing against the glass, watching me.

The weather forecast was for more snow later in the day. They said it was cold and gray outside. I could have sworn it was a sunny day in July.

So far all I knew was Friday night. I didn't know where or what time. The mall? The high school basketball game? Movies? Ice skating? Pizza? Arcade? Seven o'clock? Seven-thirty? Eight?

Was I supposed to meet him somewhere? Would he come to the house for me? When would he let me know? Where? How? At my locker? Lunch? Spanish, our only class together? Practice?

All day long, as the snow came down, I rolled a hundred questions around like jellybeans in my mouth.

He wasn't at my locker.

He stayed with the guys at lunch.

In Spanish, I said "Hi." He said "Hi" back. He smiled.

It was clear to me by then that it would happen after practice. That was the logical time. He would be waiting for me outside the girls' locker room. Or maybe in the hallway, hanging around the trophy case. He would turn away from the trophies, look at me, smile. "Hi," he would say. Or maybe, "Hi, Maisie." And then: "Listen, about tonight, here's what we're gonna do . . ."

He wasn't outside the locker room.

He wasn't at the trophy case.

So? He's still getting changed. Give the guy a chance.

Okay, so I waited at the trophy case. I waited until a scary thought occurred to me: What if Tina comes by? She wouldn't even bother saying, "Who are you waiting for?" She would just go, "Ah-hah!" She would know. I wasn't ready for anybody to know yet.

So I walked down the hallway. In a snail race, I would have come in last. I opened the school door. The snow was almost up to my knees. It was still falling. *Oh no,* I prayed, *don't let the snow spoil everything. Please.*

I went down to the street. Nobody was shoveling yet. At least I had heavier shoes on this time.

All the way home I thought I heard my name being called. I thought I heard footsteps running after me, a hand reaching out to touch my shoulder, *Hey, Maisie, about tonight . . .*

At my front door I stopped. I waited. *Don't turn,* something warned me. But I did.

It was all snow and silence and one car groping along the street.

I went in.

I was halfway up the stairs when the phone rang. John reached it first. I ripped it from him.

"Maisie?" said a voice, *his* voice.

I clamped my hand over the receiver so he couldn't hear my sobby gasp.

I mostly listened.

". . . meet me . . . Shirts Plus . . . seven . . . okay?"

"Okay," I said.

"Bye."

"Bye."

My eyes were watering. I walked into my room. Bernadette was standing. I high-fived her.

"*Yeah!*"

Chapter Thirty-one

MY FATHER DROVE ME TO THE MALL. I didn't tell him why. He didn't ask. The way things had been going lately, my parents would give me just about anything I wanted. I said I'd call when I was ready to come home.

Eric wasn't there.

Well, I was a couple of minutes early. I went into Shirts Plus and browsed around.

I hoped I looked okay. I had almost called Tina and asked her to come over and make me up. But she would have overdone it. So I locked the bathroom door and did it myself. I felt about as expert as a first-grader doing finger painting. I just did lipstick, eyeliner, and a smidgeon of shadow.

Were the Shirts Plus salesguys panting at the sight of this gorgeous creature? Well, at least they weren't fleeing out to the stock room.

There he was, veering off from the mall walkers. Jordan hightops, stone-washed jeans, cowhide jacket. Holding back the swimming pool smile, like he was going to dish it out a little at a time, not to spoil me.

"Hi," I said.

"Hi," he said.

We stood there for a while, looking at the Friday night mallers. Most were kids. Snow probably kept the old people home, but nothing keeps a kid from a mall on a Friday night. All the different jackets, school names.

"Still snowing?" I said.

He nodded. "Yeah."

We stood some more. For the first time it occurred to me that maybe he was nervous too. Shy. Tongue-tied.

"Wanna buy some shirts?" I said. I chuckled.

He didn't know it was a joke. He looked into the store, at the racks. He shook his head. "Nah."

More standing.

The way we were watching the crowd, you might have thought a parade of dancing hamburgers was going by. Let's go, Delong, I was thinking. You're the quarterback. Call the signals.

And then I thought: So what are you, Potter? Little Miss No-Mouth? I said, "Want to walk?"

He shrugged, nodded, looked over the crowd once more. "Sure." We walked.

We didn't stop too long at any one place. We checked out Herman's Sporting Goods. We shivered over a tarantula at Paws 'N Jaws. There were no rats in the store. Were they all in pet snake stomachs? I wanted to tell Eric about Bernadette, but I changed my mind.

We played a game of Crash Course at the arcade. He demolished me. That got a smile out of him, even a laugh, but he wanted to keep moving. Which was fine with me, because the best part was just the walking itself, the being together. How many times had I walked that mall before? A thousand? Now it all seemed brand-new, fresh. Places I hardly ever noticed before—Payless Shoes, Globe Travel, Candle Country—all of a sudden they were interesting, beautiful.

We saw kids we knew from school. It was fun watching their reactions. They smiled. They were friendly. They said *Hi*. But their eyes gave them away. Like, *Whoa—look who's together!*

Tina surprised me.

We ran into her and a couple other basketballers. But she didn't wave the whole mall to a standstill, point to us, and go, "Ah-*hah*!" She was cool. She just gave a little nod, a no-big-deal smile. "Hello, people," she said. She put out her index finger to be slapped. "Maisie, Eric. Nice to see you two." And she moved on.

I wondered if Eric realized what a special moment that was. I wondered if even Tina knew. She had treated us like a couple. Established. Had said *you two*. Like we *belonged* together.

Even my one and only problem was a nice one: what to do with my hand. Should I let it out in case he wanted to hold it? Or would that be too obvious? When my hand was out, it kept brushing against his. Each time I put it in my pocket, I got the feeling he had just been about to reach for it.

I was trying to get my hand problem sorted out when I noticed we had come to La Roma Pizza for the fourth or fifth time. As he had done the other times, he stopped and checked out the sample slices in the window: pepperoni, sausage, cheese-and-broccoli, you name it.

"Why don't we go in," I said. "You've been looking at those things all night."

"Not hungry enough yet," he said. And we moved on.

But I knew I had him thinking about it now, because we stayed in that wing of the mall and were never far from La Roma. Then, as we were cruising by Wee Three Records, he looked back, stopped, and said, "Let's get some."

We each ordered a plain slice. They were just out of the oven, so we didn't have to wait. Eric carried the slices, I carried the sodas. That's when I saw them, at a table in back, Lizard Lampley and my former best friend, Holly Gish.

The way we sat, Eric's back was to them. I was facing them. That didn't mean I had to look at them.

Eric made it easy not to look. His smile took me right back to the swimming pool. Up till then I had done most of the talking. Now he was blabbing a mile a minute, going on about football and wrestling and his older brother's Mustang convertible, which he had ridden to the mall in.

"Not with the top down, I hope," I said.

"I wanted to," he said with his sly-fox grin, "but my brother wouldn't put it down."

We both laughed.

"Hey," he said, "want to check it out?"

"Check what out?" I said.

"The Mustang."

"What do you mean?"

"It's in the parking lot. My brother's not leaving till nine-thirty." He thumped the tabletop, like signaling a pin. "Man, I just remembered. He's got *tapes*. We could listen to tapes. And wait'll you see the dash. Oh man!"

He pushed his chair back till he was practically in a crouch. Just his fists were on the table. His eyes were sparkling. His voice was getting louder. He was really excited.

"Let's go," he said, and started to get up.

I just sort of went up with him. I caught a glimpse of four gaping eyes as we left the table. I could feel them on the back of my neck as we headed for the entrance. Then I felt something else—his hand on my waist. He had his arm around me.

Chapter Thirty-two

T<small>HE SNOW HAD STOPPED.</small>

The key was attached to a little magnet thing underneath the car.

"Pretty sneaky," I said.

"Case he gets locked out." He grinned.

He opened the door on the passenger side and let me in. Then he got in on the driver's side. When he pulled his door shut, it was like closing the door on the first thirteen years of my life. Part of me, little Maisie, seemed still outside the car, her face at the window, peering in. The older me was in a different world, dark and leather-smelling.

He inserted the key and turned it—the dashboard leaped to life, like when my dad would say "Okay . . . ready . . ." and turn on the Christmas tree lights.

I sat in my own bucket seat, ready for launching into my own future.

Eric's voice came out of the darkness. "What do you think?"

"Wow" was all I could say.

"Listen"—he said—"presto."

Both doors snap-locked: *chuk.*

He started the engine.

"Hey," I said, "you can't drive."

He snickered. "Just putting the heater on. Feel that?"

"It's cold."

"It'll be warm in a minute."

"Couldn't we get carbon monoxide poisoning or something?"

Another snicker. "Nah. That's just if you're closed up in a garage."

He reached between the seats. Plastic cassettes clattered. He inserted one into a green-glowing slot below the radio. He pressed a button.

Music!

"Miami Sound Machine," he said with a snort. "My brother likes them."

"How old is he?" I said.

"Twenty-two."

"Must have a good job, car like this."

"Federal Express. He loads boxes."

"Oh."

We listened for a while.

"Quadriphonic sound," he said.

"Huh?"

"Four speakers. Two in front, two in back. You're in the middle of the sound."

"So are you," I said.

We listened more.

I laid my head back. I closed my eyes and let Miami Sound Machine cover me in quadriphonic sound. I wondered if this was like taking a Jacuzzi in music. He was right, it was getting warmer.

Then he was on me.

His mouth was on mine, mashing my lips against my teeth. Suddenly there were two tongues in my mouth and only one was mine. I was going down, down. The top of my head was scraping the door. One of my shoes was caught in the steering wheel. I had been in this position plenty of times recently, but it was always on a wrestling mat. Now when I looked up I saw the convertible top of a Mustang instead of the lights of a gym ceiling.

I might have done something quicker, but at first I was too shocked. Then, when I realized what was happening, I didn't want to believe it. I wanted to take it back to last summer, to the swimming pool, start it all over. I could almost hear little Maisie beating on the window: *Not this way! Not yet!*

Then his tongue was out of my mouth—and into my ear.

That did it.

I knocked his head away with the heel of my hand. He came right back, snuffling into my ear like a hog in a pail of garbage. This time I brought the heels of both hands together with his head in the middle.

He howled. He pulled back. "What are you *doing?*"

"What are *you* doing?" I yelled.

"I thought you *liked* me!"

"I *did!*"

I got my foot out of the steering wheel, but not before it blasted the horn a couple of times. I pulled myself up. Miami Sound Machine was doing a happy, snappy, dancy song. Didn't they know? Didn't they care? I groped for the door handle, took a year to find it. It wouldn't move.

"Unlock it!" I screamed.

He pressed a button.

Chuk.

I was out, racing across the snow and slush to a phone, calling my father, "Now, I'm ready, yes, now, *now!*"

It took forever for my father to get there. "More snowplows than cars on the road," he said. A basketball game was on the radio.

Tank was in the living room, along with P.K. and my mother. Overnighting again. They all looked at me kind of funny, like they were waiting for me.

That's crazy, I thought, they couldn't know what happened.

I went upstairs. John was at the bathroom mirror. He glanced at me, then quick-turned away, like he was shy or something.

I headed for my room. There was only one rat left in my life now. At least it was the good one, the one I could really talk to.

I turned on the light. I didn't see her. Was she hiding under the cedar chips? I ran over.

She was gone.

"Bernadette!"

"Tank didn't mean it, Maisie."

I turned. They were all in the doorway. They still had that funny look.

"He made a mistake," said P.K. "Didn't ya, Tank?"

She had her arm around Tank's shoulders. Tank's eyes and mouth were three round shapes. He nodded.

"What are you talking about?" I demanded. "Where's Bernadette?"

We all stared at each other for a while, them in the doorway, me in my room.

My mother said, "She's gone."

I shrieked.

P.K. started babbling and bawling.

"They were playing with her downstairs," my mother said.

I couldn't believe it. "*Downstairs?*"

"Well, yes, you can blame me for that. They asked. I said it was all right. So . . ." She took a deep breath. The rest came out like a recital. "They were playing downstairs. They wanted to see if Bernadette would like some snow. P.K. opened the door to get some snow. I might mention that at the time I was upstairs. The door was open. Bernadette got loose"—another long breath, a shake of her head—"and went out the door."

She had one hand on P.K.'s shoulder, one on Tank's.

"Nobody *looked* for her?" I said.

"They ran to me," my mother said. "This was just before you called. I tried looking outside with a flashlight—"

I punched Bernadette's empty house. "Great."

P.K. wailed, "It wasn't Tank's fault, Maisie! Don't be mad!"

"Yeah, right," I snarled.

I tore off my jacket and whipped it across the room. It hit my desk lamp and sent it crashing to the floor. P.K. and Tank huddled against my mother. "Hey, why should I be mad? I just go through the worst night of my life and come home to find my rat gone. What's there to be mad about?" I was storming around the room, kicking everything in sight. "I want my rat! You had no right to take her outta here!" I raised my leg and kicked my desk with the bottom of my foot. I jabbed my finger at Tank. "It *was* your fault!" I was going to say the same thing to P.K. but I never got to it. I saw the look on Tank's face and felt like ripping my tongue out.

And then P.K. was charging, jumping up at my finger and kicking my shins. "Let'im alone, you big goof! You big goof!"

My mother called, "Hey!"

She was looking down the stairs.

Tank was gone.

I could hear him running down the steps. I could hear the front door opening.

"Tank!" P.K. screamed.

Everybody moved. I moved the fastest. I passed them at the bottom of the stirs. I shot out the door.

He was running down the driveway, or maybe wading is the word. His little legs sank almost to his thighs with every step.

He turned and headed down the sidewalk, where the snow was just as deep. The neighborhood wouldn't be shoveling till next morning. Except for my father's tire trenches, the snow was level as a shelf from front yard to sidewalk to street.

I went to the sidewalk. I stopped for a second. I almost just wanted to watch. He was so cute, galloping in slow motion through the snow, like a bug in a sugar bowl.

From the house my mother's voice: "Boots!"

Did she mean me or him? Neither of us wore boots. Or a coat. But the snow came higher on him. And I had yelled at him, the little kid who wouldn't go to sleep one night until I picked him up and hugged him.

Down at the end of the block, twin headlight beams, higher than usual, swung onto our street.

I started after him.

I trotted. The snow dragged my legs. Long strides. I must have looked like those astronauts bounding over the surface of the moon.

Tank didn't have the power to slash through the snow with just his legs. His whole body turned from side to side with every step. Back and forth, like a paddle.

The lights of the snowplow made the snow shine. I could hear it. I had never noticed the sound before. I didn't like it. So different from a car. Not a go noise. A push noise. A here-I-come noise. A get-out-of-the-way noise. A growl. A grunt.

A grumble.

Tank was five or six houses away now.

I ran.

"Tank!"

The snow vanished under my feet.

He was gone.

Poof.

One paddle turn to the left, and he never turned back. Veered behind . . . a parked car . . . the Andersons' Bronco . . .

Did he stop?

Did he stay?

Did the snowplow man, up in the cab of the snowplow, looking down at all that snow in the headlights, did he—could he—see the tiny little person without a coat behind the Bronco . . .

Dashing out from the Bronco!

"TANK!"

I flew.

The street was blazing. The snow was grumbling.

He was in the light, but not his face, because he had his back to the light, his arms outstretched, the plow like a huge white wave . . .

And then he was in the dark, he was *under* the light . . .

I reached him an instant before the plow.

I scooped him up.

The plow scooped us up.

He clung to me. "Let go!" I screamed. I pried his fingers from my neck. His legs were wrapped around me.

"LET GO!"

Turning, twisting, churning.

Screams.

I grabbed a fistful of his shirt in one hand and held him at arm's length. With my other hand I wrenched his legs from me, and with one hand on his shirt and the other on an ankle, I heaved him to the side as far as I could.

Land in snow, I prayed.

And then I was riding the grumbling avalanche alone.

Chapter
Thirty-three

I WAS ROLLING. I thought, *How far is he gonna plow me?*

There were lights overhead.

Was I being pinned?

"She's awake," a voice said.

Another voice: "Oh thank God . . . thank you."

Sounded like my mother.

"Mom?" I said.

"Maisie?"

It was my mother. There she was. Her face.

I stopped rolling. My mother's face went away.

"Mom!"

"I'm here, Maisie. I'm right here."

"What's going on?"

"You're at the hospital. You were hurt."

"The snowplow?"

"Yes. But you're all right now. You're all right."

I was being lifted. It was like being in a hammock. It was fun. I wanted to swing. But then I was down again.

"Mom?"

"It's okay, Maisie. They're taking care of you."

Somebody was shining a tiny light into my eye, a star come to visit me.

"Mom . . . Tank?"

"Tank's . . . fine, Maisie. Perfect."

Her voice broke up, like she was crying.

"What's the matter, Mom?"

She sniffled. "Nothing. Not now. Tank is in the waiting room with Daddy and P.K. and John. You . . . you saved him."

Then a man's voice was asking her to leave, saying she could come back soon, but now they had some work to do.

That's about when the pain started.

"Bernadette!" I called.

There was no answer.

Tank had landed in a pillow of snow. Not a scratch on him.

The snowplow driver hadn't seen us. It was my parents' screams that stopped him. By then he was nearly to the end of the block.

I wasn't on the plow. They found me in front of the Tolivers', packed in snow like a flounder at the Acme. I was unconscious. My father wanted to take me to the hospital himself. He figured that would be faster than waiting for an ambulance to make it through the snow. Somebody had a better idea. I rode to the hospital in the snowplow.

When they finished with me in Emergency, they figured I got bonked in two places: my head and my ribs. My head hurt only when I was awake and my ribs hurt only when I breathed or moved. Other than that, I was pain free.

They kept me in the hospital over the weekend. Because of my ribs—they called them "bruised"—I had to lie on my back. It was murder at night, because I'm a stomach sleeper. Only my parents were allowed to visit. Time dragged.

I went home Monday morning.

P.K. and Tank were waiting. P.K. tried to jump on me but my mom caught her in midair.

I looked down at Tank. "I'm sorry, Tanker. I didn't mean to yell at you. I was having a bad night."

"That's okay," he said. He was grinning. He brought his hands out from behind his back.

I shrieked, "Bernadette!" And then I shrieked again, because shrieking was a no-no to my ribs.

My mother led me to the sofa and helped me sit down. Tank put Bernadette in my lap. I bent down as far as my ribs would let me. Bernadette stood up. She put her tiny hands on the end of my nose.

"She was in the mailbox," my mother said. "Don't ask me how."

Our mailbox is on the wall of the house by the front door. The wall is brick.

I picked Bernadette up. She sat in my hand. I grinned like a proud mama. "She could do it," I said.

"The mailman found her," my mother went on. "Saturday. He

knocked at the door. He handed me the mail with this funny look on his face."

P.K. chimed in. "And he says, he says, Mrs. Potter"—making her voice low—"I hate to tell you this, but there's a *rat* in your *mailbox!*"

We all howled. I howled twice. My mother winced. "Uh-oh . . . kids, let's try not to say anything too funny for a while."

"So Mommy said don't tell Maisie till she gets home," said P.K., " 'cause you might get too essited." She turned to my mother. "Was that too funny, Mom?"

My mother bit her lip and looked at the ceiling. "Oh no . . . no."

Around lunchtime, Mr. Cappelli came over. In my living room, he didn't seem like a coach or teacher. He sat beside me on the sofa. He had a big brown envelope in his lap.

"Almost every Raven stopped by to see me this morning," he said. "Asking what happened, how you're doing. They said to say hello, get well fast."

"Not Kruko," I said.

He laughed. "Even Kruko."

He put his hand on mine. His face got serious, like a father. "We're all very proud of you, what you did. They said tell her we'll miss her."

My eyes were getting blinky. "Hey," I said, "they won't miss me for long. I'm gonna be back in a couple of days, next week at the latest. Doctor said."

He pointed to himself. "*This* is the wrestling doctor. I say you're through for the season. There's only four matches left."

"Coach, I gotta be there for Parents' Night."

Parents' Night was the last match of the year. Maybe the last one of my life.

"No way," he said.

"If you don't let me, I'll cry."

He laughed. He opened the big brown envelope and brought out a folded square of silky material. "Hold this end," he said. He walked halfway across the living room with the other end, unfolding the team motto banner that had been hanging on the wrestling room wall. Only now there was something new. An extra word had been sewn on:

"Hang it on your wall," he said.
I didn't cry until he left.

On my bed upstairs I found a note. It wasn't signed. It didn't have to be:

> I'm glad you're my sister.
> I never really wanted a brother.

Tina went around to my teachers and brought my homework. She also brought *The Evening Post* in from the front step. She held the paper high and spun around, showing the world. "Ta-dah!"

I couldn't believe it was the *front* front page, not the front sports page.

STUDENT BECOMES HERO
IN SNOWPLOW RESCUE

Tina called everyone into the living room and read them the article.

When all the fuss was over and we were alone again, she said, "Guess it didn't work out with you and Eric, huh?"

"Guess not," I said. I thought for a second. "How would *you* know? He blabbing at school?"

"No," she said. She looked sheepish. "You really want to know?"

I told her I did.

"Well, they're back together."

"Him . . . and Lizard?"

She nodded.

I shrugged.

We stared at the rug for a while. A long while.

She said, "So, is it worth it?"

"What do you mean?" I said.

"Wrestling. Is it worth it to you now, with him out of the picture?"

I looked at her, but I didn't have the answer.

Chapter Thirty-four

Well, Mr. or Ms. Editor, at long last I'm coming to the end. You have to admit, when I write a Letter to the Editor, I don't mess around. I started this back in March, after the wrestling banquet, and here it is almost time for the new school year. Blame it on my mother. Remember, back in Chapter 28, she was the one who suggested it.

Seriously, I realize you can't print all of this. You probably won't even read it all. That's why I stuck the Post-it on the first page, telling you to skip right to Chapter 34 if you wanted. Because if I had to pick one chapter to get printed, this would be it.

The other thirty-three, they talk about stuff most people know about by now anyway (except maybe what my physical and my first weigh-in were like). But this chapter is about that picture you ran in *The Evening Post* after our last match on Parents' Night. The picture showing the team carrying me off the mat on their shoulders after I lasted three full periods with the kid from Oakview and barely lost, 7-6.

The picture that showed the crowd in the background giving me a standing ovation and me all happy and whooping it up and throwing my arms in the air.

That picture.

And the caption that went with it, that said, "Maisie Potter, responding to the cheers of the crowd . . ."

The caption was wrong.

I don't mean this to sound ungrateful or anything, but if you want to know the truth, it wasn't the crowd that I was responding to. Not really.

Don't get me wrong, I was glad to hear the cheers. I was glad I didn't hear any "Ba-BAWLLLKs!" I was glad that nobody threw safety pins and that some people even threw flowers. Believe me, I was glad for all that. It made me feel good.

What I'm saying is, even without all that, I still would have felt good.

I'm saying, it was nice to get the people's approval, but by the time they got around to giving it to me, I didn't need it. I already had the approval of the person who counted most.

Me.

You see, you get a really great view from the shoulders of your teammates. You can see things clearly that maybe weren't so clear before.

The first faces I picked out when I looked down belonged to Eric Delong and Liz Lampley. (I don't call her Lizard anymore.) Smiling up at me, arm in arm, together again. I was happy for them. I was even happier for me. Because I knew—finally and for sure—the answer to Tina's question.

Yes, it was worth it.

YES.

And I looked at the people—standing, cheering. How many of then had written Letters to the Editor?

I didn't care.

I had lost Eric Delong.

I had lost every bout that wasn't forfeited to me.

I had lost my best friend.

According to the Hunkiest Boy poll, I had lost my sex.

According to some of the letters to you, I had lost my soul.

But I didn't feel like a loser.

I felt like a winner.

I *was* a winner!

So, Mr. or Ms. Editor, if you don't have room to print this chapter, maybe you can at least print the picture again. If you do, would you be kind enough to correct the caption as follows:

Maisie Potter, responding to her victory, keeps the cheers of the crowd and respectfully returns their approval. When asked how she managed to get through the season, Miss Potter laughed and said, "Hey, when you're undefeated, it's easy!"

Sincerely,

MAISIE KAY POTTER

Related Readings

Eric Anderson

Just Another Wrestler

This newspaper article tells the story of a girl very much like Maisie, who excels as a wrestler on the boys' team.

SOME WILL CALL Nella Bernadoni a trailblazer. Inevitably, some also will say the Darlington High School freshman should not be doing what has become second nature to her.

Bernadoni isn't tangled up in all the labels and philosophies; she just wants to be like everyone else on her team.

"I just consider myself another wrestler," she said.

While Bernadoni, 14, is the first girl to make the varsity squad for the Redbirds, girls are increasingly common on prep wrestling teams. Last year, nearly 3,000 girls competed on boys teams across the country, including about 100 in Wisconsin.

But Bernadoni is one of the most talented girls to hit the mats in this state.

As an eighth-grader last season, she finished fifth at 106 pounds in the high school division of the United States Girls Wrestling Association national championships. This season, she is ranked fifth at 106 pounds by the USGWA and 10th at 103 by Female High School Wrestler.com.

"I'm definitely anticipating that she will be productive over her four years," Darlington coach Tom Mathias said.

"Technique-wise, she's a good-looking freshman. She's got things to learn and she's got time to mature . . . but I would tend to think that by the time she's done she could be the best female wrestler from the state of Wisconsin. That's maybe a lot of pressure to put on a freshman, but that's what I think of her."

Wrestling at 103 pounds, the 5-foot-1, 100-pound Bernadoni has a 5-2 record with four pins for the Redbirds.

One of those pins came in Friday's 36-33 win over state-ranked Fennimore, which was Darlington's first Southwest Wisconsin Athletic League Division 2 dual-meet victory in five years. She won the Silver Division title at the Waunakee Invitational last weekend with a 3-1 record—all of her victories were by pin—and went 3-0 to win a junior varsity tournament earlier in the season.

"I don't look at her as male or female; all along I've looked at her as someone who can help the team," said Mathias, who has coached Bernadoni in the Darlington youth wrestling program for seven years.

"We have had a hard time filling the lower weights, so Nella was a godsend. She can fill one of those spots and get some wins for us, and even if she doesn't win, she probably won't get pinned."

In wrestling, teams receive six points for a pin, six points for a forfeit and three points for a decision. "Even if I do get pinned, it's still just the points lost for a forfeit," said Bernadoni, who counts her older brothers, senior Jeve and sophomore Silas, as teammates.

"The team accepts her really well, pretty much nobody has any problem with her. Everybody has been pretty supportive," said Jeve Bernadoni, a 135-pounder for the Redbirds. "We're glad to have her."

Bernadoni had some foes choose to forfeit rather than wrestle her during junior high school competition, but she hasn't encountered any protests from opponents in high school. Before the season, Mathias took aside Bernadoni and 119-pound junior Barb Richards, who is on Darlington's junior varsity team, and told them they might run into some awkward situations.

"I told them they're in a male-dominated sport and they're going to have to work twice as hard as anybody else, be better conditioned, work on building strength, because there's not one boy out there that wants to lose to them," he said. "(The boys) are either going to be afraid of them or they're going to want to crush them. That's just the way it is."

For Bernadoni, having Richards to practice with has been helpful, despite the weight difference. "This is the first time I've ever had another girl to practice with," Bernadoni said.

And it appears more girls are getting involved in wrestling. Three other Wisconsin girls are nationally ranked, and Bernadoni will likely face another girl, Prairie du Chien junior Holly Lange, in a dual-meet tournament at Prairie du Chien on Jan. 13.

"I think there are a few more girls every year," said Bernadoni, one of about 10 girls in the youth program in Darlington. "I don't know if it will ever be its own sport, but for the bigger girls, I think if they knew they would only have to wrestle against girls, they might do that more.

"If there was girls wrestling, I think a lot of weight classes could be filled. Right now at the bigger weights, girls don't go out because they know they would get killed."

And in a strange twist, that would be something that might take Bernadoni a little while to get used to. After all, she's always wrestled boys. "I've always considered it normal. Last year, it was a big change to wrestle against girls," she said of competing in the national tournament in Michigan.

Of course, she wouldn't mind having more girls out there with her.

"I'd say to (other girls), go ahead and try it," she said. "You're only going to get positive things out of it, and it's a wonderful thing."

Mary Pemberton

68 Teams Compete in Iditarod

The same winning spirit that drove Maisie to distinguish herself as a wrestler drives the participants of the Iditarod, the 1,100-mile dogsled race in Alaska.

ANCHORAGE, ALASKA (AP)—Doug Swingley, the only non-Alaskan to win the Iditarod Trail Sled Dog Race, now will try to become just the second musher in history to take it three years in a row.

The man from Montana has plenty of competition in the 1,100-mile marathon from Anchorage to Nome. This year's field consists of six previous champions, including the big three who have won all the races since 1992: Swingley, Martin Buser and Jeff King.

Sixty-eight teams will line up Saturday in downtown Anchorage for the ceremonial start of the Iditarod, first held in 1973 to commemorate a dash to Nome in 1925 to deliver lifesaving diphtheria serum during a disease outbreak. The real racing begins Sunday.

The top 30 finishers will share a $550,000 purse. The winner gets $62,857 and a new truck. Swingley will try to match the feat of Susan Butcher, who won from 1986-88. Both have won four times overall, with Swingley getting his first victory in 1995.

Swingley took the lead halfway through the 1999 race. Last year, he finished in nine days, 58 minutes to trim his own record by more than 13 hours.

It's hard to know what Swingley will be bringing to this year's race, and that's just how he likes it. He lives and trains near his home in Lincoln, Mont. He likes keeping his Alaska competition guessing.

"If the opportunity is there, this team certainly is capable of winning," he said.

The buzz this year is about King, a three-time Iditarod winner who finished third last year. King won the Kuskokwim 300 and the Tustumena 200 mid-distance races this year. Mushers use those races to tune their teams for the Iditarod.

King, who drew the first slot out of the chute on Saturday, said this year's team is fast enough to overtake Swingley's.

"They're awesome," he said.

While Rick Swenson—the only person to win the race five times—hasn't taken the Iditarod since 1991, he's made a strong showing this year, finishing second to King in the mid-distance races.

Swenson is hoping for some good luck this year. Given the talent now in the race, it takes a near-perfect run to win, he said.

One of his dogs was seriously injured last year after it was spooked by people on the trail and ran into a tree. Veterinarians saved the dog's life.

Last year's second-place finisher, Paul Gebhardt scratched in two mid-distance races this year, but says his dogs are ready now for the Iditarod.

"It was a tough training year," he said. "Everybody's back."

DeeDee Jonrowe won the Copper Basin 300 mid-distance race in January. She predicted the team that finished 20th last year will place in the top five this time.

"I've had no injuries. I think the team is really prime," she said.

Jonrowe had finished in the top 10 every year since 1998 except for 1999 when she was in fourth place before scratching because her team quit.

Derek T. Dingle

Breaking the Color Barrier

When Maisie joined the boys' wrestling team, she helped to break down some gender barriers. Five decades earlier, an African American baseball player named Jackie Robinson helped to break down the color barrier when he joined a white baseball team.

As Jackie was making a reputation for himself as a sensation in the Negro leagues, he dreamed of breaking the color line in major-league sports. Jackie had always believed that the demonstration of excellence would show that blacks were qualified to take advantage of opportunities in American society. That is why he worked so hard to become a skilled athlete in college and a hard-driving leader in the Army.

He also knew the disappointment of being overlooked. In 1945, Wendell Smith, a sportswriter for the *Pittsburgh Courier*, then the nation's largest black newspaper, used his influence to get Jackie and two other Negro league stars a tryout with the Boston Red Sox. For years, black sportswriters such as Smith and Sam Lacy of the *Baltimore Afro-American* had been trying to pressure major-league baseball to recruit from this untapped wellspring of talent. But like this mock tryout, their efforts produced no immediate results.

Back east in New York City, someone else was also thinking about integration. Branch Rickey, the president of the Brooklyn Dodgers, decided that it was time to hire from this bumper crop of stellar athletes. The choice was extremely personal for Rickey. He remembered that in 1910 when he was a college coach at Ohio Wesleyan, he could not register one of the members of his team—a black man—at hotels when they were on the road. The indignity that the player suffered stuck with Rickey for more than forty years.

Rickey started sending scouts to Negro league games, telling the press he was recruiting an all-black team to play when the Dodgers were away. The reports came back about a number of top-notch black ballplayers—Paige, Gibson, and Bell among them—but the one who stood out to the cigar-chomping Rickey was the hard-hitting, swift-running shortstop for the Kansas City Monarchs—Jackie Robinson.

Rickey needed a player with a college education and the courage to bear verbal—maybe even physical—abuse without striking back. He believed that Jackie was his man.

On the hottest summer day in August 1945, Jackie and the Dodgers' scout, Clyde Sukeforth, went to the team's headquarters in Brooklyn. Jackie recalled the conversation he had had earlier with Clyde. "Branch Rickey is interested in you. He wants to meet you in New York," Clyde had told him. Jackie had just shrugged. Negro league players did not expect much from the major leagues. But now that he was riding up to the fourth floor to meet one of the most revered men in baseball, Jackie started to sweat. And it was not because of the weather.

After some small talk, the imposing Rickey said in his deep, booming voice, "I am interested in you as a candidate for the Brooklyn Dodgers of the National League. I think you can play in the majors. What do you think?"

Jackie was stunned. He could not utter a word. Rickey continued, "You think you could play for Montreal, our minor-league team?"

"Yes," Jackie said simply.

After making Jackie the offer, Rickey asked, "Have you the guts to play, no matter what?"

Jackie answered, "I can play the game, Mr. Rickey."

Rickey explained, "Well, this is what's going to happen. White people all over America are going to see a black man play against, and even more importantly, *with* white men. Many of them are not going to like it. You are going to get letters filled with hate and fear. Some may even threaten you."

"Mr. Rickey, do you want a ballplayer who is afraid to fight back?" Jackie asked.

"Mr. Robinson, I'm looking for a ballplayer with the guts enough *not* to fight back. Because the only way for a black man to break the color line is not to retaliate." Then Rickey whispered, "Three years, Mr. Robinson. Three years. That's what I'm asking you. At the end of those three years, I give you my word you can say and do what you want. Because, if you do what I say, there will be more and more black players in baseball."

Jackie looked into Branch Rickey's eyes. "Mr. Rickey, I've got to do it." The two shook hands. It was a handshake that would change baseball—and America.

Breaking the Color Line

Before he could suit up in an official Dodgers uniform, Jackie first had to prove himself in the minor leagues. Minor-league "farm clubs" are where new professional players improve their skills until they are ready for the big leagues. Jackie was slated to play for the Montreal Royals, the top farm team for the Dodgers.

Spring training with the Royals was rough for Jackie and Rae, whom he married after he signed with the team. They had to go south to Daytona Beach, Florida, where the team prepared for the season. As they left to go to the airport to catch their flight, Mallie gave Jackie and Rae a shoebox of fried chicken. Even though they were embarrassed by the stereotype that Mallie's offering conjured up, they took it as they departed.

Their troubles started when their plane arrived in New Orleans. The Robinsons were not allowed to get on their connecting flight or to eat in the cafeteria. The only meal available to them was Mallie's chicken. When the Robinsons reached Pensacola, Florida, the next day, Jackie and his wife were forced to sit in the back of the bus. Rae quietly cried as Jackie pledged not to fight back.

Jackie was not greeted by the welcome wagon when he arrived in Florida. His teammates avoided him. The team was not permitted to play in an exhibition game in Sanford, Florida, because it was against the law for whites and blacks to play together. But Jackie had endured tough trials and he thought he could get through this one. His first game was in Jersey City. As the Montreal Royals got set to play the Jersey City Giants, Jackie took his position as a second baseman. The sun shone brightly on spacious Roosevelt Stadium as band music played and the fresh smell of hot dogs and peanuts filled the air. The 25,000–seat stadium was choked with more than 51,000 people.

Thousands of black fans came out to root for Jackie. In the top of the third inning, the Giants' pitcher tried to sneak a fastball by him. Jackie drove the ball over 340 feet for his first home run. The crowd exploded in cheers, even though he was playing for the opposing team. He smiled as he saw Rae in the stands. But his grin grew even broader as his teammates came to congratulate him and welcome him to the team. Later in the game, Jackie stole two bases. Beaming Branch Rickey said of Jackie's first game: "That's a pretty good way to break into organized baseball."

Led by Jackie, Montreal won the International League pennant in the Junior World Series that season. It was not an easy season for Robinson, who faced racial taunts from opponents, baseball fans, and even his own team. Jackie wanted to confront his tormentors but remembered his promise to Branch Rickey. He met his detractors with grace and dignity. Performance overcame prejudice, and Jackie was named Most Valuable Player in the league. The bigger reward for Jackie was being mobbed and cheered by the fans who didn't seem to care that he was a black man, but just a great ballplayer.

On April 9, 1947, the Dodgers issued a press release announcing that they had signed Jackie Robinson to suit up as a major-league player. As in the past, Jackie had to prove himself all over again.

Breaking the color line and entering the majors was no easy feat. Jackie's signing was announced two years before the military was integrated, eight years before school desegregation, and a decade before the start of the Civil Rights movement. Jackie's face had been plastered in all of the newspapers as the first African-American to play major-league baseball this century. Reactions to his signing to play for the Dodgers were mixed. Many questioned his ability to play. Wearing his neatly pressed blue-and-gray wool uniform—number 42—Jackie took on a heavy burden, knowing that he had to succeed.

Jackie did not receive a warm reception from all of his teammates. Shortly after Jackie joined the Dodgers, his teammate Eddie Stanky walked up to him.

"I want you to know something," Stanky said, pointing his finger at Jackie. "You're on this ball club and as far as I'm concerned that makes you one of twenty-five players on my team. But before I play with you I want you to know I don't like it. I want you to know I don't like you."

Jackie stared right back into Stanky's eyes and replied in a calm, steady voice, "All right. That's the way I'd rather have it. Right out in the open."

Other team members—many of whom came from the South and had never interacted with African-Americans as equals—circulated a petition protesting Jackie's new slot on the Dodger team as a first baseman. Rickey uncovered the ringleaders and scolded them individually, asserting that anyone who was not willing to have a black teammate could quit.

The cold shoulder he received from his team was nothing compared to the abuse he received from opponents and spectators. Pitchers threw lightning-quick pitches at his body when he stood at the plate. Players would slide into Jackie's base with the spiked heels of their cleats aimed high. On the field, he withstood jeers, boos, and insults, and in the locker room, he received threatening letters. With hostility from his opponents and little support from his teammates, Jackie got off to a poor start in the major leagues. In his first four games, he went to bat twenty times without a base hit. Many were saying that Jackie was not ready for the big leagues. Discouraged, Jackie thought the same thing. Burt Shotten, the Dodgers' manager, called him aside. "Jackie, you're putting too much pressure on yourself. I won't take you out of the lineup. Relax and the hits will fall."

Jackie's next game was against the Phillies. The Phillies' dugout hurled insults at him every time he came up to bat. Ben Chapman, the Phillies' big, tobacco-spewing manager, told his players that "there was a $5,000 fine for anyone who didn't go after Robinson." And they did just that. He could hear the jeers from the Phillies' dugout. "Nigger, go back to the cotton fields," cried one. "Go back to the bushes," yelled another. When Jackie went out to bat, the Phillies sent a black cat out to home plate.

Jackie was starting to crack. How long can I remain patient? he asked himself. Then Jackie decided to strike back—on the field. Jackie hit a single. He also stole three bases, including home plate, winning the game for the Dodgers. When Jackie received further verbal abuse from the Phillies, he discovered that he had a surprising new defender: his teammate Eddie Stanky. "Why don't you yell at somebody who can answer back?" Stanky shouted at the Phillies in defense of his teammate.

Jackie's stellar play earned him the respect, admiration, and friendship of his teammates. Jackie was a power hitter, batting .297

and knocking twelve home runs out of the park his first year. He ranked second in the league in runs scored. And he could run: Jackie bunted for nineteen hits and led the league with twenty-nine stolen bases. His efforts helped the Dodgers beat the St. Louis Cardinals to win the 1947 National League pennant. Many of the naysayers who thought Jackie would not last his first season voted for him to be Rookie of the Year. At the end of the season, more than 26,000 fans crowded into Ebbets Field to salute Jackie. Throughout the season, new attendance records were set in Brooklyn, Philadelphia, Pittsburgh, Cincinnati, and Chicago. Wendell Smith wrote: "Jackie's nimble / Jackie's quick / Jackie's making the turnstiles click." Jackie's detractors were starting to turn around. In fact, by the end of the season, Phillies' manager Ben Chapman said, "Robinson is a major leaguer in every respect."

Although the Dodgers did not win the World Series that year, Jackie realized a greater victory—two other black ballplayers signed major-league contracts. Dan Bankhead joined the Dodgers, and the Cleveland Indians signed up Larry Doby, the first black to play in the American League. In fact, Jackie paved the way for pitching legend Satchel Paige. The old barnstormer finally made it to the majors with the Cleveland Indians and, in 1948 at the ripe age of forty-two, became the oldest rookie ever to play professional baseball. Jackie's dream that the major leagues would be fully integrated seemed like it might finally come true.

Lucille Clifton

jackie robinson

*Many words were used to describe Maisie when she
joined the boys' wrestling team. Lucille Clifton tells of
Jackie Robinson's triumph quietly and in few words.*

ran against walls
without breaking.
in night games
was not foul
but, brave as a hit
over whitestone fences,
entered the conquering dark.

from
Knots in My Yo-yo String

Jerry Spinelli

In this chapter from his autobiography, Jerry Spinelli writes about the different memories he and his older brother have from their childhood.

WHEN MY YOUNGER BROTHER became student council president as a ninth grader at Rittenhouse Junior High, I was proud. In the years that followed Bill and I played golf, flung Frisbees, shared friends and cars. We were pals.

But those days were yet to come. During the George Street years, the four-and-a-half-year difference in our ages ruled out being pals. When I was in fourth grade, Bill was in kindergarten; when I was in tenth, he was in sixth. We had different friends, different involvements. Except for two years, we attended different schools. We shared parents and a house, but that was about all.

Because I wasn't paying much attention to him then, my store of memories today is not nearly as well stocked as I would like it to be. I remember him, when he was very young, eating ashes from the coal furnace.

I remember him pilfering my penny collection to buy an ice cream cone.

I remember him as a toddler, packing our first puppy, Spot, into our father's black-domed lunchpail. When this kept happening, Spot was sent off to a family without toddlers.

A few years later along came Lucky (so named because after the lunchpail puppy, we were lucky to get another), part terrier, part unknown, a pretty mutt, mostly black, with white chest and paws and tip of tail. She was friendly, eager, barely disciplined, which is to say, she was like my little brother. They got along wonderfully.

I remember feet-fighting in my bed—lying on our backs and flailing our feet at each other. It was just harmless, boy horseplay, but sometimes I carried it far enough so that Bill wound up crying. I think now that in making him cry, I was fabricating an outlet for tender feelings toward my little brother that found no expression in the natural course of events.

I remember Bill getting into trouble more than I, both at home and in school. I secretly admired him for daring to just do things, regardless of consequences.

And I envied him his animation. Well before I entered junior high, I began cooling out. Gone were the days when I would serenade passersby from the gate in my yard or jingle-jangle off to school in my cowboy outfit. I was still friendly, but in a shyer, quieter way. Meanwhile Bill was just lighting up. He was everything I was not: bold and lively and funny. He was a natural mimic and a clown. He had, as the Lloyd Price song went, "Personality."

And that's about it, the extent of my kidhood relationship with my brother, Bill.

Or so I thought.

For something surprising happened, something nice, when I told him I was working on my autobiography. I invited him to jot down any recollections of me that he might have, in case I missed any. Several weeks later he handed me a list of memorable moments. I read it over. I was stunned: I hardly recalled any of them.

He remembers his own hurt feelings when I wouldn't let him ride my tricycle.

He remembers, as a preschooler, how impressed he was that I could read cereal boxes.

He remembers how angry I got when he raided my closet for shirts and when he tangled the strings of my Howdy Doody puppet.

He remembers fearing for me when Raymond Chillano beaned me with a pitch during a Knee-Hi baseball game. And when the same Raymond Chillano, knowing I could not swim, tipped me in my street clothes into the deep end of the pool at the Valley Forge Swim Club. (Raymond was not always so hard on me. In fact, he was one of my best friends.)

He remembers an episode which, at the time, he considered positively historic. I was in the fifth grade at Hartranft Elementary. Bill was in first. Normally we walked the three blocks home for lunch. But on this particular day our mother had to be somewhere else, so she gave me money and told me to take my brother somewhere to eat. We met at noon. We went to a luncheonette a block away. We ordered our lunch, and for a little while Billy Spinelli felt as big as anyone in that place. He was having lunch in a restaurant, not a parent or teacher in sight, off into the world with his big brother. On the way back to school we were chased by bees.

Bill remembers as clearly as I the dirt path by the railroad tracks. He especially remembers one day when I propped him on the bar of my Roadmaster and gave him a lift from the dead end to the park. He remembers feeling the carnival-ride thrill of it. He remembers feeling proud and special. Most of all he remembers feeling safe, his brother's breath in his ear, his brother's arms joining the handlebars in a protective embrace.

Such are Bill's recollections, and after all these years they bumped me over to a new point of view. I have always tended to see our relationship from a single perspective, from my own eyes; that is, Bill as my little brother. Now I see it from a second perspective: myself as his big brother.

I have decided that I like Bill's memories of us better than my own. I especially like the one about the bike ride on the dirt path. I am picturing it now. I am feeling Bill's feeling of safety, and I am feeling the big brother in myself. Maybe, if I keep picturing this memory of Bill's and feeling it for a long-enough time, it will begin to fool me into thinking it is my own.

Naomi Long Madgett

Offspring

These two poems express the need and the struggle to reach beyond one's boundaries to find out what truly makes one happy.

I tried to tell her:
    This way the twig is bent.
    Born of my trunk and strengthened by my roots,
    You must stretch newgrown branches
    Closer to the sun
    Than I can reach.
I wanted to say:
    Extend my self to that far atmosphere
    Only my dreams allow.

But the twig broke,
And yesterday I saw her
Walking down an unfamiliar street,
    Feet confident,
    Face slanted upward toward a threatening sky,
And
    She was smiling
    And she was
    Her very free,
    Her very individual,
    Unpliable
    Own.

Mary Oliver

The Journey

One day you finally knew
what you had to do, and began,
though the voices around you
kept shouting
5   their bad advice—
though the whole house
began to tremble
and you felt the old tug
at your ankles.
10   "Mend my life!"
each voice cried.
But you didn't stop.
You knew what you had to do,
though the wind pried
with its stiff fingers
15   at the very foundations—
though their melancholy
was terrible.
It was already late
enough, and a wild night,
20   and the road full of fallen
branches and stones.
But little by little,
as you left their voices behind,
the stars began to burn
25   through the sheets of clouds,
and there was a new voice,
which you slowly
recognized as your own,
that kept you company
30   as you strode deeper and deeper
into the world,
determined to do

the only thing you could do—
determined to save
35   the only life you could save.